FORTRESS OF THE GOLDEN DRAGON

FORTRESS OF THE GOLDEN DRAGON

A
Persian
Tale

Inspired
by the
Shah-Nameh

Homa A. Garemani

HAMPTON ROADS
PUBLISHING COMPANY, INC.

Cover design by Grace Pedalino
Cover digital image © 2004 GettyImages/PhotoDisc/Hisham F. Ibrahim

Hampton Roads Publishing Company, Inc.
1125 Stoney Ridge Road
Charlottesville, VA 22902

434-296-2772
fax: 434-296-5096
e-mail: hrpc@hrpub.com
www.hrpub.com

If you are unable to order this book from your local
bookseller, you may order directly from the publisher.
Call 1-800-766-8009, toll-free.

Library of Congress Cataloging-in-Publication Data

Garemani, Homa A., 1935-
Fortress of the golden dragon : a Persian tale inspired by the Shah-Nameh
/ Homa A. Garemani.
    p. cm.
ISBN 1-57174-418-5 (alk. paper)
I. Firdawsei. Sheahneamah. II. Title.
PS3607.A74F67 2004
813'.6--dc22

                                    2004019443

ISBN: 1-57174-418-5 (pbk)
ISBN: 1-57174-453-3 (cloth)

10 9 8 7 6 5 4 3 2 1
Printed on acid-free paper in the United States

nce in a land far away there was a small town called Kolallan. High mountains protected this peace-loving community from its unfriendly neighbors on the north side, whereas in the south, azure blue hills attracted travelers to linger. Hundreds of pomegranate trees adorned prairies surrounding the land. When ripe, their sumptuous fruit cracked, displaying ruby seeds which satisfied the most discriminating taste. At night delicious oranges lit orange groves like fiery globes illuminating the landscape. Tall palm trees decorated every house. Their branches stretched out together like umbrellas, protecting the households from summer's blazing heat and fanning out the hot air. The dates produced were the finest in the world, but their juicy and delicate nature made exportation beyond the town impossible. Along the roads, lotus trees and myrtle gracefully provided shade to weary travelers. Deep wells were the source of clear cool drinking water for the town.

In spite of all the natural resources, the people of Kolallan were poor. Their main source of income was from cotton fields. Strangely, the male population was only half as many as the female. The elders believed that a few decades ago a witch had put a curse upon the town because a group of maidens had refused to serve her food and drink.

"Without husbands you shall be spinning until your hair turns white like cotton," the witch had declared.

In fact, all the maidens of Kolallan occupied their time by gathering cotton buds, spinning, and weaving in order to save money for alluring dowries.

The people of Kolallan were good-natured and fun loving. In spite of their meager income, a month never passed during which they did not celebrate and enjoy themselves. Doors were never locked and they made strangers feel welcome to share their simple meals. Domestic animals were used only for their milk and wool. The occasional source of meat was from hunting game, which was usually shared by many households. Every morning groups of cheerful maidens carried their spindles to the hills, shared each other's lunch, and sang songs. This ancient hymn was always the first they chanted:

> O glorious queen of heavenly spring!
> All water from your motherly water flow.
> Part of water you make stand,
> Part of water you forward flow.
> A thousand lakes you possess,
> A thousand rivers you own.
> Your brightness carried by horses four,
> All white, of the same blood,
> The wind.
> The rain.
> The sleet.
> The cloud.
> And thus upon the earth rising,
> Snowing, sleeting, hailing,
> Crushing down hates of all hatred,
> Destroying the wicked.
> O glorious queen of heavenly spring!
> You are life increasing and heavenly!
> You are herd increasing and heavenly!

Maidens of barren wombs will beg of thee:
Grant them children of males pure in seed,
With words kind and good in deed.
O glorious queen of heavenly spring!

In the evening they returned home to deliver their spindles to their parents.

Among the maidens, the fairest of all was Allusin. With beauty and grace, she was tall and slender, with long, soft, curly hair the color of fresh dates. Her teeth were cotton-white, her cheeks as rosy as pomegranate seed, and her eyes sparkled with joy, even in sad moments, like sweet oranges at night. Her voice was crystal clear, like the water of deep wells.

Her constant companion was a white sheepdog given to her by a man traveling on foot who had stopped by their house years ago asking her for a cup of water. He had worn a long turquoise blue robe down to his ankles, and a wide leather belt with seven rows of stitches in seven colors around his waist. He carried a dragonhead staff.

It was a Wednesday, the thirteenth day of the month, and Allusin was nine years old at the time. She gave him a cup of cold water and began to pet his dog affectionately.

"What a pretty collar!" she said, noticing his neck. It had two narrow braided cotton ropes in purple and red entwined, with nine tiny lapis lazuli stars hanging from it. "What is his name?" she asked the stranger.

"His name is Saiparak," said the man in a low voice as he looked at her with piercing eyes. His face and his hands were bleached white, as were his hair and beard. "It is the name of a bright star in the sky," he continued. "A magic star! Each month, for ten days the star turns into a tall young man fifteen years of age. For ten days it becomes a bull with golden horns, and for ten days it appears as a white horse with ears and reins of gold. It is the staunchest foe of the black dragon with no wings and no tail. He seems to be taken with you. Perhaps you care to keep him?"

"Oh yes!" she said with great excitement. "May I?"

"Of course," he replied softly as he left.

"What is your name?" Allusin called after him.

Without looking back he answered: "Peerbabu."

There were myths and legends about Peerbabu in neighboring towns. Rumors were that he had lived more than a thousand years and had been in his mother's womb for seventy-two years. He was born with the bleached-white skin, white hair, and very long fingernails. His father, a cobbler, believing his newborn son to be evil, left him on a high mountain to be ripped apart by vultures, but a gigantic bird with the combined faculties of bird, beast, and human found the baby, fed and raised him. Her nest was on an island in the middle of a vast ocean. It rested upon a tree, which bore the seeds of all trees. The legend was that whenever she flew away a thousand branches grew out of that tree, and when she sat a thousand branches broke and seeds of all kinds scattered into the ocean.

Peerbabu lived on a hill in a three-story tower shaped like a cross. Each level had windows on all sides. A small garden surrounded the building, with a short waterfall on the west side. It flowed to the east through a small stream and down to a cliff. The tower was hidden by tall trees and was not visible from outside unless one could find his way up through a winding narrow passage, ending at a wide terrace upon which the tower was built. No one remembered ever having seen the interior of the tower.

Peerbabu was known for his healing powers. People from faraway towns and villages brought their terminally ill and left them under an old oak tree at the foot of the hill by his house. If they were gone the next day it was a sign that the person had a chance to be healed; otherwise the patient died. After they were healed, patients returned home with no memory of their healing process.

Peerbabu was frequently seen going to the mountains, where he stayed out of sight for days and perhaps months. Old villagers said that they had seen him riding on a white rhino with a horn as long as ten cubits. Some whispered that he could order the wind to carry him to the most remote parts of the world. People revered him, but feared him as well. Therefore, they kept their distance.

Allusin took good care of Saiparak. When she ate bread, she gave him three mouthfuls, too. She never gave him hard bones or leftover food. Saiparak, with his short tail; long, narrow head; long, rough hair; and pointed nose was a sheepdog with the character of a shepherd. Watchful and a light sleeper, he was the first to leave the house in the morning, and he tailed Allusin when she came home in the evening.

On the north side of the town of Kolallan were two castles, not far apart. One castle belonged to a young prince whose immediate family had been killed by nomadic tribesmen in an ambush when he was only an infant.

In the other castle lived Prince Sarabaress, the young prince's only uncle.

Prince Sarabaress had deep-set, light brown, melancholic eyes; a high forehead; and was tall and slender. He had the attitude and the mentality more befitting a philosopher than a royal prince. He had no children of his own, as his beloved wife had died at childbirth. Devastated by the news of his twin brother's death, instead of planning a vengeful attack, which was commonly expected of a prince, he had decided to go into seclusion and dedicate his life to writing. One week after the event though, when Peerbabu showed up at his castle, his plan took a new course. Peerbabu was carrying a baby who was wrapped in the royal white blanket bearing his family emblem, a rosette. Peerbabu handed the baby boy over to Prince Sarabaress.

"Here is the sun prince to shine in your life!" said Peerbabu.

Shocked, Prince Sarabaress checked the prince's birthmark. On the back of his left shoulder there was a red jagged circle with a black mole in the center.

"He is Prince—"

Prince Sarabaress was about to declare the name of the prince when Peerbabu interrupted him, "His name should not be spoken until he has passed adolescence and has built enough inner strength to withstand dark forces. The name has special resonance that, if picked up by such force, may cost him his life now. The attack on his family's camp was an attempt to destroy the little prince."

"Will there be a sign as to when it can be revealed?"

"You will know when the time comes."

"Then I will declare that he will be called Prince Athar. My brother chose this name for him when the prince was born. But one week later, during the official ceremony to initiate the baby as his heir, my brother called him by the other name. I believe the name was suggested by the astronomers."

"Astrologically it was the right name but after his family was murdered, the situation changed."

"You must tell me how he has survived!"

Peerbabu said that in his dream he had seen the tribesmen entering the camp and had rushed to the scene, but had only been able to rescue the infant prince. He waited one week for Prince Sarabaress to go through grieving and until he was certain that it was safe to make the infant's survival public.

"Peerbabu, you never cease to amaze me!" said Prince Sarabaress, clasping the baby to his chest. "I was heartbroken when my wife died and my infant son, who bore the same birthmark, did not survive. When the prince was born, I felt somehow that I was being compensated for the loss. Then, last week, with the death of my brother's family, I lost faith in even the divinities. But look now! Here I am with the biggest gift of all. I should pray for enlightenment to receive divine guidance in educating this blessed baby."

"Our little prince needs the care of a woman now. Do you know of one who could feed the baby?" asked Peerbabu.

"I have a trusted friend whose wife gave birth to a baby boy named Barzin. He was born on the same day as the prince, only twelve hours later when the sun was setting. I am sure that she will be delighted to feed two," said Prince Sarabaress.

The expression on Peerbabu's face changed. A sudden and unexpected wave of sadness that covered his face alarmed Prince Sarabaress.

"Oh, Heaven!" said Prince Sarabaress. "Concealed in vast happiness is grieving, and from the depths of sadness sprouts joy." His tone had lost its glee.

"Such is the world," said Peerbabu as he was leaving.

Therefore, as was the custom, the prince and Barzin lived with women until the age of seven. Then they were trained by the army officers to learn the arts of war and were tutored by teachers in the fields of philosophy, history, and religion until they reached adulthood. All their activities were under the constant and direct supervision of Prince Sarabaress.

Unlike the prince, Barzin was not a healthy child and was often bedridden for weeks. The prince was very protective of his friend who was in poor health. To defeat Barzin in games and sports, boys had to pass the prince. Whenever Barzin was ill, the prince spent hours at his bedside telling him the events of the day and new weapon techniques that he had learned. He cheered him up by making fun of those who were not their favorites. The prince and Barzin grew up together as close brothers.

One spring day the prince and Barzin were hunting far from the prince's castle when they heard singing. Quietly they got off their horses, walked to the hilltop, and hid behind trees so they could listen to a group of young girls who were sitting in a circle in front of looms, weaving. Their faces were bright and cheerful and their braided hair dangling on each side of their breasts was the sign of maidenhood. The prince and Barzin waited until the maidens finished their song. Then slowly they walked toward the girls. Saiparak was already at the prince's side wagging his tail.

"Good morning, ladies!" said the prince.

Startled, the girls looked up and saw two young men approaching them. One had light brown hair and deep hazel eyes and was holding the reins of a black and white stallion. A royal emblem adorned the saddle. The other man, with dark brown eyes and dark brown curly hair, had a dapple-gray stallion. Shy and surprised, the maidens began to giggle.

"Very strange!" thought Allusin. "Saiparak is greeting the young prince. How does he know him? I do not remember ever seeing him before, yet his face is familiar!"

"Whose dog is this?" asked the prince, as he petted the dog.

"He is mine," said Allusin, as she stood up and walked toward Saiparak, who was joyfully jumping up and down around the prince. When she got close to the prince she knelt down.

"Calm down, Saiparak!" She held the dog in her arms and looked up into the prince's eyes. She felt a warm breeze embracing her body. She blushed and her heart began fluttering. There was a feeling of joy she had never before experienced.

The prince sank into her eyes. He felt drawn to the exquisite maiden who was looking at him with admiration. He had been used to receiving love and attention all his life, but he was not quite certain about his own affections for others. He often asked himself if his love for Barzin's mother was the same as Barzin's love for his own mother, or if the respect that Barzin had for his father was the same as he had for his uncle. But at that moment with Allusin, all doubts were erased from his heart, as if instantly his soul had acknowledged that what he felt was love. To him it felt like the moonlight entering his room and lighting up dark corners to assure him that no monster was hiding there.

"What did you call him?" asked the prince.

"His name is Saiparak," said Allusin. "He is very particular and sometimes is not friendly at all. If he did not like you, he would not have run to you."

"I am honored!" said the prince, bowing in a courtly manner to the dog. His gesture made the maidens laugh. They gathered around the two young men, showering them with questions. Unlike Barzin and the others, who were engaged in conversation, the prince and Allusin became pensive and quiet. The prince gently held her hand and pulled her aside. Their pulses and the rhythm of their breathing became harmonious.

"It may sound strange," said the prince, "but in the flick of an eye my world has changed. It is as if the illusionary life I had before has disappeared in your eyes. And now, just by holding your hand, the real world has come into existence. I need to talk to you in private. May I accompany you home?"

Allusin nodded and softly smiled.

"What time do you usually leave this place?" asked the prince.

"Before the sun goes down," replied Allusin.

"Where should we meet? I do not want to lose you."

"Down the hill somewhere," said Allusin. "Do not worry! Saiparak can always locate you. He is good at finding people for me, especially the ones he likes."

When the girls packed their spindles to go home, Allusin left her friends and said, "Saiparak, go and find the prince! I will follow you."

The prince was waiting for her down the hill. As they strolled, they talked like old friends and told each other stories about their families and friends. When they reached an orchard, Allusin turned to the prince and said, "I leave you here because I must go home now."

"May I see you next week?" asked the prince.

"You may," replied Allusin.

"Right here would be a good place to meet."

"Then I shall be here in one week's time. But still I do not know your name, my prince."

"My name is Athar. But yesterday, in my father's library, I came across a document in which I read that he had named me . . ." At this moment the prince paused as if something held him back from pronouncing it out loud. So he whispered it in Allusin's ear. Allusin repeated it, exclaiming, "What a beautiful name!"

Both were astounded by the way the name echoed through the hills. It was the first time that the prince had heard his name being spoken. It had strange resonance in his ear and brought about a chill, which crawled under his skin and made him shiver. His immediate reaction to the unfamiliar feeling was to hold Allusin in his arms and kiss her on the lips. They embraced for a long time. Gradually the warmth of her body and the excitement of the moment made the chill disappear, so when they departed, he forgot about the incident.

2

The next day as Allusin left home, she saw Peerbabu. Saiparak rushed to him and began to lick his sandals. Peerbabu petted him.

"He remembers me. Dogs are faithful, are they not?"

"Especially this one. I remember you too, Peerbabu. You gave me this dog." And after a pause she asked, "You are not going to take him away, are you?"

"Of course not, my friend," said Peerbabu. "What is given with good intention should never be taken back. As a matter of fact, I brought you another present. Soon you shall become fourteen. I want you to have this ruby ring as your gift. You should wear it at all times, and never let anyone else wear it. Remember to look at it every morning to notice if there is any change in its color."

"It is a beautiful ring; but Peerbabu, what do you mean by the color changing?"

"When a dark force is active around the person who wears this ring its color becomes darker. It gives the person a warning; but you need not be frightened, just stay alert! You can rely on this ring because it never lies. I must leave now."

Allusin put on the ring and called to him as he was leaving, "Peerbabu!"

He stopped but did not turn.

"Why do you never look back?" asked Allusin.

"Does the wind ever look back?" answered Peerbabu.

And like the wind, he swiftly disappeared into the heavily wooded land.

As she passed through the orchard, where she had said goodbye to the prince, she said, "Saiparak, it was right at this spot where the prince and I kissed, do you remember?"

Suddenly an apple from a tree fell at her feet and Saiparak began to bark. She looked around but saw no one.

"Keep quiet, Saiparak! Sometimes you bark for no reason at all. It is silly to bark at a fallen apple. You lose people's trust. But do not worry! I shall always love you no matter how silly you act. You are a good dog!"

She picked up the apple and cleaned it with the sleeve of her gown. She bit into it and broke the apple into halves. A tiny white worm was inside. As she was gently removing the worm she heard a warm voice very much like Peerbabu's. "If you keep me in your box, I will make you weave fast like the wind."

Allusin hesitated for a second, but the idea of weaving so fast appealed to her. If she could weave faster she would make her family very happy. So she put the worm into her spindle box. When she began to weave, she realized that the spindle on the loom was spinning faster than before.

During lunch she said to her friends, "Have you noticed how fast I am spinning today? I knew I would."

"How so?" Doeshat asked. "I have not noticed anything."

Doeshat was the daughter of the mayor. She had never liked Allusin but tolerated her because she was engaged to Allusin's brother, Vantu.

Allusin said, "I found a worm in an apple. I took it as a good omen! It may have magical properties—a gift from heaven for my upcoming birthday!"

"Maybe it means that apple was rotten!" Doeshat said, and the others giggled along with her.

"It is only a worm, you silly!" Doeshat continued. "If it were magical, it would never have remained a pitiful worm. It would have turned itself into an eagle, a dove, or a raven. Everybody knows that you are stupid and clumsy. Why should heaven send you anything?"

But at the end of the day Allusin returned with fat spindles, surprising her mother.

"I do not believe this! How did you manage to weave this much?" asked her mother, Visseh.

"A worm helped me," Allusin replied excitedly. "There was a little worm in an apple that dropped at my feet today. I felt it was a good omen, so I kept it in my box. Something else, Mother. I also saw Peerbabu today. Do you remember him? He was the one who gave Saiparak to me. Look! He gave me this ring."

Visseh looked at the ruby ring and said, "Old people say strange things about Peerbabu. I have never seen him myself, but he must be a good man, because he is very kind to you."

Allusin's father, Adaddera, rushed to Visseh and grabbed the ring to examine it.

"This is an expensive ring. Real gold and real ruby," said Adaddera, his eyes lighting up. "We should use it as your dowry to find you a husband. I wonder why he takes so much interest in you. No one gives away anything without expecting something in return, but I see no harm so long as he is good to you and brings you gifts like this ring, which is a much better gift than that disobedient dog. When one believes something is a good omen, it may well become a good omen. We shall see. If it proves to be true, we all should take good care of it."

Adaddera was short and stubby with a sunburned complexion, thick curly black hair, large nostrils, questioning black eyes, and a cunning smile. He was by nature a suspicious and contradictory man. When focused, he had a quick problem-solving mind, but his pleasure-seeking body often caused him trouble. His skill at flattery, which made him popular among women, and the ensuing adulterous affairs caused many quarrels with his wife. He did not have deep religious convictions but always daydreamed that someday, by some miracle, he would be rich. So, when days ended without any significant event he became disappointed—a frustrated man, caught in conflict between his greedy nature and extreme laziness.

That night the ruby ring and the story about the worm brought him great comfort and hope. Though he tried to conceal his feelings from his family, his immediate change of attitude toward Allusin was obvious. He did not let her wash the dishes and promised her a new dress.

Allusin was glowing with happiness. Nobody in the family had ever treated her kindly. She was not the favorite child. Her brother Vantu was the eldest, and she was the youngest, and in between the two, three boys had died within days of their birth. Her mother was a kindhearted but emotional, superstitious, and insecure woman. She loved her husband, and putting up with his infidelity made her weep in bed for hours. Whenever Allusin was harassed by her father or her brother, Visseh flared up and said to her:

"Women are cursed, I tell you! If you were a boy they would not have treated you this way, and I would not have to worry so much. The best I can hope for you to marry is a buffoon like your father. Men do not fall for quality in a woman. They are after money and position, of which we have neither. How am I going to find you a husband? What am I to do if you cannot get a man?"

From early childhood Allusin had helped her mother with the household chores. Because of Visseh's intense irritability her husband never criticized her for the things that displeased or angered him in the house. Whether a water jug was broken, the cupboard was not dusted properly, or the meal was tasteless, the blame was always on Allusin.

In spite of Visseh's objections, Adaddera had made Allusin begin weaving when she was only four, to add to the family's income. Instead of resisting or complaining, Allusin used to sing in a low voice, as if she were reaching deep inside her for comfort. In her forgiving nature Allusin demonstrated a great tolerance for false accusations. She rarely defended herself, but no one could push her over the edge. Once when she was thirteen, she stood up to her older brother. On that occasion Vantu kicked Saiparak and tried to make him leave the house, yet Saiparak stayed put and barked violently at him. Vantu had reached for a stick to beat away the dog when Allusin placed herself between them and yelled:

"Do not dare raise a hand against this dog! Saiparak will never leave me! If I tell him to kill you, he will tear you to pieces in a second. If you kick him again I swear I will order him to do so."

Vantu was shocked by her unexpected fierce response and immediately retreated. From that day on he made a conscious effort to ignore the dog's unfriendly manner toward him.

Vantu was spoiled by their mother and had adopted many of his father's weaknesses, including his laziness. He made snap judgments and was quick in withdrawing when confronted with force. With his good looks and charming attitude Vantu had stolen the heart of the mayor's daughter, Doeshat. He was expecting that the marriage would bring him comfort and leisure time. Vantu was always rude to Allusin, but since she had begun to add a noticeable amount to their income he treated her more gently.

Allusin could not wait to tell the prince all about the magical worm and how it had changed her family's attitude toward her, but the next week, before she could share her happiness with him, the prince had disturbing news for her.

"I am summoned by King Vima to take part in some forthcoming battles. Unfortunately I must leave tomorrow. I want you to know that this separation is temporary and upon my return we will be married. I want you to wear this."

With that, the prince put a jade pendant around her neck. It was set in gold and had a loop on top through which a gold chain ran.

Allusin embraced him. "My prince, when I hear the thunder of your horse approaching, my unhappy feelings flee. When I see the lightning of your sword removing the thorns along my path, all my doubts are cut off as well. My heart has already stopped singing, but in your absence the hope of seeing you again will be stronger in my heart than the sorrow of missing you. How long will you be gone?"

"I am not sure. It may take months or even years to defeat the enemy. Whilst I am away you can receive news from Vestur, the high priest of the temple. He is a good friend of my uncle and can be trusted. He will give you the news if you go to the temple."

"Then I shall go to the temple every day," said Allusin. And as she was embracing him she continued, "Last week I found a worm in an apple and I wove a hundred times faster. It was the happiest time of my life. I had you, my family was kind to me, and I thought nothing sad or bad would ever happen in my life. Today you are going away and the magic of the worm may vanish tomorrow; but as long as I have the hope of you returning to me my heart shall survive."

Allusin put the worm in a wooden box and each day fed it a small piece of apple. As the worm gradually grew in size, they built larger boxes for it. Bigger containers were made of elaborately carved polished wood, which were then replaced by ivory boxes lined with satin and velvet. Over time the worm developed a new saffron color on its skin, and it refused to receive food from anyone except Allusin. No one dared to get close to it if Allusin was not around, as it would squirm and screech. Therefore, she became the sole custodian of the worm, and against her wishes, she had to stay home. She missed her friends and their singing but was pleased by the attention she got from her family and friends. Since she had nothing else to occupy her time except to go to the temple and chat with the high priest once a week, she worked until dark. She wove so fast that the spindle seemed to be standing still, producing mountains of thread each day that was carried away on a hundred mules.

Adaddera's house was crowded with young men of high stature proposing to Allusin, but she refused them all, saying she had no intention of marrying anyone. Adaddera was delighted by her decision, believing that if she went to another house his fortune would reverse. So she was left safe with her secret love for the prince.

Adaddera became enormously rich, prominent, and influential. He built a huge house outside the town and hired many servants. People gave him the title of "Septabliss," meaning a person with seven heavenly blessings. They believed that bliss was bestowed upon him by the seven heavenly bodies. More than anybody else, Septabliss himself believed it to be true. At last the long-awaited miracle had happened and his dreams of glory had come true. Within a few months he became a changed man. The ability to order people around gave him deep satisfaction and the relief of not forcing himself to go to work early mornings brought him great pleasure. When he tasted how powerful the money had made him, he could not stop himself from demanding more. He enjoyed spending money to buy people's affections and respect. Receiving expensive gifts from her husband, even Visseh did not seem to mind his affairs as much. People put him on a pedestal upon which he was elated to stand.

Little by little, as people heard the story of his fortune, they came from Kolallan and many of the neighboring villages, bringing offerings to Septabliss's house and praising the worm for its benevolence. Septabliss rewarded them according to the generosity of their offerings. He helped them to resolve their financial difficulties and develop their businesses by using their expertise; in return he demanded a share of their future profits. Gradually cotton fields were expanded, foreign laborers were hired to do the job that previously had been done by the maidens, and on the pastures grazed thousands of cattle and horses. The community engaged in exporting linen, wool, horses, and oxen to the neighboring lands and faraway countries.

The quiet town of Kolallan spread in all directions and grew into a boisterous, densely populated city with shops, peddlers, well-dressed men on horses, and women in carriages who lived in big houses with large flower gardens, conscious of their wealth and social status. Musicians and dancers, jugglers and acrobats were brought in to entertain guests at parties and festivities. As Kolallan grew, it attracted the best artisans, traders, and artists. As the male population grew, eligible maidens found strong young men for husbands and bore many children.

The wealthy families adopted a discriminating attitude about whom to invite to their homes and whom to deny the privilege of their company. Unless the visitors had lofty positions they were not received. Gradually the sense of harmony and closeness diminished in the community. Their diet also changed: assorted meats and spices became part of their daily consumption. People became suspicious of travelers who lingered long in their town. There was a sense of resentment about the rapid growth of the foreign population and the changes that newcomers brought about with their own customs. High walls were built around houses to protect the inhabitants against an increasing number of armed bandits, and locks were put on doors to keep thieves out. The wealthier citizens even hired guards to stand at their gates to keep strangers out, or to sit in watchtowers to guard against robbery. The transient security of wealth left a long-lasting insecurity in their lives.

In the beginning, Septabliss, believing he was blessed by the Heavens, gave great financial help to the high priest, Vestur.

Vestur was a learned man approaching his old age, respected and liked by the people. He was kindhearted, compassionate, and humble, but his trusting nature affected his judgment and often made him prey to clever predators.

He enlarged the temple of the Mother Goddess, the Lady of Immaculate Waters, and made it look more appealing to the eyes of visitors. Marble columns were raised and the altar was decorated in gold. Its new, enlarged library contained hundreds of texts, maps, and books.

He designated a large building to accommodate orphans, as well as fatigued and famished poor travelers who entered the town looking for jobs. He also established a big budget for priests to travel abroad to familiarize themselves with the cultures of faraway lands and to broaden their minds by taking part in discussions with learned people of other faiths.

Vestur had visited the worm during its early development and had found it to be harmless, accepting the idea that it was a heavenly gift sent to help the town of Kolallan. Gradually though, he noticed that people were paying visits to Septabliss's house more often than they went to the temple. The rapidly declining number of visitors alarmed Vestur. Consequently, one day he sent for Septabliss to discuss the matter. Septabliss's reaction deeply disappointed him. He realized that Septabliss considered himself to be the source of bliss rather than a man who was blessed and was totally consumed by his own grandeur; the worm was a veil he was hiding behind.

From that day on, Septabliss became more displeased with Vestur's projects and privately began to criticize him, cutting down the budget he had allocated to the temple. Septabliss wanted to be recognized as the gracious and benevolent one, not the high priest. He wished to eliminate Vestur, but he did not know how to make it happen.

3

ne night Saiparak yelped all night long. Allusin tried in vain to calm him, saying, "Keep quiet, Saiparak! It is midnight. There is no reason for you to be upset. Are you going through your moods again? You silly dog! Go to sleep!"

But the dog kept moaning all night long.

In the morning when Allusin looked at her ruby ring she noticed that the stone's color had changed to a darker shade. She was disturbed and went to feed the worm. When she entered the worm's room she was terrified to find that two more heads had grown out of the worm's body. Its soft shiny skin had turned black and crusty and was covered with small thorns. She felt like screaming, but her paralyzed throat did not make a sound. Horrified, she ran to Septabliss.

"Father, the worm has changed! It has three heads now!" she said, her voice trembling with fear.

Septabliss was still in his bed looking pale and sick. It was the fourth night in a row that he was having a recurring nightmare. He saw himself walking in a wasteland under the blazing sun with his tongue out, panting like a dog dying of thirst. He saw a caravan passing in the distance, and he made several attempts to shout to catch its attention, but there was no strength in his voice to carry the sound beyond his body. The words dropped from his chin like a wall tumbling down. Fatigued, he began to crawl on the sand, dragging his body forward. He did not get far.

Exhausted, he thought that perhaps by digging he might reach water. With what small force was left in him he began to dig. Suddenly his fingers felt wet! Excited, he dug deeper. Bubbles of thick muddy water surged up. He was exuberant, waiting for the water to clear, but its thickness never changed. The flow turned into a rushing river carrying him away like driftwood. He struggled to keep his body afloat, but the rising waves reached a whirlpool and pulled him under.

Each night he woke up, sweating profusely. His skin was itching from head to toe, and he felt a great thirst in his throat and a crippling hunger in his stomach.

It took Septabliss a few minutes to collect his thoughts and focus on the terrified face of his daughter. He rushed to the worm's room to see for himself. Indeed the worm had three heads! Instead of two soft hazel eyes it had six threatening red eyes and scruffy, prickly black skin! Septabliss gazed in shock at the worm, wondering how to react.

"Is my luck changing?" he thought. "Am I going to lose everything? Am I going to die? Or perhaps Heaven is testing me! Once Vestur said that the chosen people must go through terrifying trials to prove themselves worthy of receiving heavenly gifts. I am Septabliss! I have received seven gifts. I must be the chosen one! Then this is a trial for a higher position. I should take myself more seriously. Certain messages are conveyed only to special people, Vestur said. The worm must be merely a vehicle for my blessings, yet until people accept me as such this deformed body must be hidden at all costs."

"Something is wrong, Father, is it not?" asked a worried Allusin.

Septabliss, having recovered from his anxiety, locked the door and held his daughter in his arms.

"No. Not at all, my dear," replied Septabliss with a smile. "There is nothing wrong, I assure you. Our worm is just growing. A worm with three heads is still a blessing from heaven. With two more heads we will have three times more gold and be wealthier than ever. As long as I am here nothing will change."

"You believe so, Father?" asked Allusin doubtfully. "But Peerbabu told me that the ring—"

"Hush, my girl!" Septabliss interrupted. "No more talk of Peerbabu! He is an idiot, merely a nosy magician who is constantly interfering with the affairs of others. He knows nothing of heavenly bliss."

He paused for a second, but as he immediately felt that what Allusin had been about to say might have been important, he questioned her, "What did Peerbabu say about the ring?"

Allusin decided not to mention what she had been about to say. "He just said that no one else should wear this ring but me."

"Why?" Septabliss asked.

"He did not say," Allusin replied, looking at her ring.

"Anyhow," continued Septabliss, "I shall consult with Vestur. He is the one who can direct us wisely. But until then, this new development should be hidden from everyone, lest our fortune change into a curse. From now on this door should remain locked at all times, and no one will be allowed to visit the worm! No one except you and me, not even your mother or your brother, you hear? It is your holy duty to keep tight lips. You are blessed with this sacred secret. It is not to be revealed in any manner until Heaven tells us so!"

"I understand, Father. I will keep the door locked, but when will you consult Vestur?" asked Allusin. There was a desperate quality in her voice.

"Soon, my daughter. Soon," replied Septabliss, as he left in a hurry.

In spite of her father's assurance, Allusin was deeply troubled by the recent changes. The worm looked ugly and angry. The luster in its eyes had turned to menace. But she obeyed her father's instructions, trusting that the high priest Vestur, to whom she always confided, would make the right decision.

Septabliss summoned one of the council priests named Amaease. Amaease was fairly new in the temple. His appearance was as strange as his character. He had a triangular head, which was very large in proportion to his body, and he had narrow, piercing gray eyes under high thick eyebrows. He was short and had a big belly, but he was a strong man, a fast walker, and a boastful talker.

Amaease's father was a poor cobbler. A quiet and melancholy man whose humble attitude towards his well-to-do clients Amaease detested. Amaease did not like his two elder sisters either; and they hated him, believing that he had caused their mother's death when he was born because his head was so big. As a child he was extraordinarily thin and was always hungry, searching for food. He stole food from shops and open markets, from smaller children, and from old people in the street. At night he slept on the kitchen floor, close to the fireplace in which no fire burned. He often got up to steal some bread to nibble in silence. He was accustomed to being regularly beaten by his sisters and by many shopkeepers and even by strangers. There was a look of fear in his eyes that made him appear guilty, so he was punished for many things which were not even his fault. The cobbler was the only person who never raised a hand against him, and once in a while gave his son his own food portion. That was Amaease's childhood memory of kindness. When he was twelve he left home with a cleric by the name of Ayar who was traveling with a caravan that was passing through Amaease's town. Amaease told Ayar that he was an orphan, had no place to go to, and had not eaten for days. Because of Amaease's undernourished body and his hungry eyes, Ayar had believed his story.

Out of compassion Ayar took him in and nourished both his body and his mind. Amaease proved to have an extraordinary ability to memorize information of all sorts and systematically categorize it in his mind. He had an enormous thirst for reading and stayed in libraries and temples for weeks and months, going through books and manuscripts. He transformed his insatiable hunger for food into a thirst for collecting data on the people he met and on the places he visited. He was an artful liar and a great imposter, successfully using the information he collected to impress his audiences and to exploit situations to his advantage.

Amaease did not care for women and he abstained from other pleasures of life that usually attract young men. But when it came to money and power he was unable to control his greed. On these two subjects he never agreed with his master. He traveled along with Ayar to many countries, learned several languages, and served him patiently for many years. At the age of twenty-five he knew more information than most preachers he encountered. But to Ayar, Amaease's craftiness and his antagonistic behavior were disappointing. The more Ayar tried to bend him, the more obstinate Amaease became. He resented the poor, never hesitated to humiliate the uneducated, and always flattered the rich. He was a single-minded person who lived by his own code of conduct and had no remorse for his vile actions. Arrogance was his constant companion. Ayar never suggested that Amaease become a minister, and Amaease never cared to be one. He felt superior to almost all the subdued vicars he met and scorned their unassuming behavior.

Little by little, traveling lost its fascination for Amaease, who was tired of serving old Ayar. An urge was growing in him to find a place where he could promote and establish himself as a leader. He was confident that he possessed all the necessary qualities.

One day he left Ayar without a farewell and started a cross-country search. When he heard of the magic worm and the wealthy people of Kolallan, he said to himself that such a town must be a suitable place for him.

He introduced himself to Vestur as an experienced preacher who had served in many temples at home and abroad, using Ayar's credentials as his own. Vestur was getting old and was overwhelmed by Amaease's vast knowledge, as were the other priests of the temple. Vestur gave him the position of one of the high counselors and shared with him sensitive issues of the temple. But later, when Amaease began to reveal his ambitious nature, Vestur subtly tried to keep him at a distance.

Amaease regarded Vestur as ineffective and scorned him for not using his influence to promote the business of the temple and to fill the treasury with more gold. From the moment Amaease met Septabliss it became clear to him that he was the man he had been searching for all his life. Because of Septabliss's lack of information, his limited worldly experience, and his ostentatious manner, he became the proper target for Amaease.

As a priest it was easy for Amaease to lure people into giving him detailed information about the whereabouts of Septabliss at any given time. In a short period he found out the background of everyone associated with Septabliss and coordinated his time with Septabliss's daily plans, cleverly managing to show up at places where it was most suitable to meet him.

Amaease never missed a chance to get Septabliss's attention by praising him, or by artfully revealing his discord with Vestur.

Septabliss found Amaease impressive. Amaease's constant veneration made him feel confident, and his vast problem-solving knowledge made decision-making much easier for Septabliss. Therefore, on the day the metamorphosis of the worm occurred, Septabliss knew that Amaease was the right person to approach.

"I have watched you for a long time," said Septabliss. "You are a man with high principles, and you are far wiser than Vestur. Vestur is becoming old and somewhat senile and cannot serve the prosperous people of Kolallan anymore. People believe that the appearance of the worm was a divine occurrence and his name should be mentioned in our prayers. They firmly believe in the worm's heavenly nature. Vestur refuses to acknowledge it as such, though the temple benefits from its blessing more than any other organization. Did you hear about what happened to our neighbors last year when locusts swarmed the fields? They are still struggling hard to recover. They came to me for help. It could have happened to us were it not for the worm. Do you agree?"

"I could not agree more," said Amaease, pleased. "I have been on the road most of my life and have seen changes in rituals and prayers everywhere. Vestur is a feebleminded and old-fashioned priest whose teachings no longer appeal to people. He is only good for listening to the poor and comforting peasants. He convinces them that by the sufferings endured in this world they will be rewarded in the next, something I have never believed. The young people especially are fed up with his style. Religion must be suited to the needs of the masses. He spends most of your generous donations on orphans who should be working in the fields to earn their own living. He spends an enormous amount of money on the newcomers who soon will turn this prosperous town into a vast poorhouse."

Gratified, Septabliss said, "I am glad that we speak the same language, because we are going to need each other's support. I have a plan to remove Vestur from his position and for that I need some specific information, which probably is not available to the public. Since I am not an initiate in the order of the priesthood, what you tell me should be held in absolute secrecy. May I perhaps count on your help?"

"I trust no man more than I trust you," answered Amaease, trying to hide his joy. "I am at your service. I assure you that I can handle it without making Vestur or anybody else suspicious. What is it that you wish to know?"

"You see, today Allusin told me," said Septabliss, "that the worm is changing into a dragon. It has legs and a growing tail; strangely, it has become very sensitive to the light, and more than ever now it reacts harshly to anyone approaching it other than Allusin—even hearing my footsteps made him restless. Allusin had to close its window and we sent away all the visitors."

Septabliss continued, "Some time ago Allusin told me about a dream she had of a woman who told her of the upcoming changes. I did not pay any attention to her then. But now I know that it was a prophetic dream. Today I asked Allusin about the dream, but she did not quite recall the description of the woman whom she saw in her dream. I am going to Vestur to ask him for a proclamation so we can keep people away without disappointing them. You know how fussy Vestur is about these sorts of things. We may have to stop the visitations for some time. Can we use Allusin's dream to convince Vestur to write such a proclamation?"

"In other words," said Amaease, "you want me to tell you the exact description of the Mother Goddess, yes?"

"Exactly!" said Septabliss, embarrassed, because his foxy manner did not fool Amaease.

"It is very unusual!" said Amaease. "Dreams such as your daughter's have such deep effects that people never forget. They remain very vivid in one's memory. What else do you want to know?"

Septabliss became more uncomfortable realizing that lying to Amaease was very difficult.

"What else do I need to know?" asked Septabliss.

"Plenty!" said Amaease. "Do not worry! I will prepare you well for that meeting."

Although Amaease knew that Septabliss was lying about Allusin forgetting the details of her dream, he did not pay any attention to it. He was glad that the opportunity for him to seize power had appeared much sooner than he expected.

4

The next day Septabliss paid a visit to the high priest, Vestur.

"Last night Allusin had a strange dream," said Septabliss. "She revealed it to me this morning and I said I would come to you right away for interpretation. I do not know what to make of it."

"Of course, my dear friend. That is why I am here. What was her dream?" asked Vestur with his usual kindness.

"There was this beautiful lady in a gown made of beavers' skin," began Septabliss, pretending to be searching his memory.

"It shone with the full sheen of silver and gold. She was wearing a golden necklace and square golden earrings. Yes, Allusin definitely said square golden earrings. I thought it was unusual, but that is what she said."

Vestur bent forward with rapt attention. "Go on! Go on!" he urged.

"She had an eight-cornered crown upon her head with a hundred stars," continued Septabliss. "At each corner was a ray in the shape of a wheel. Then the lady spoke to her."

"She spoke to her, did she?" asked Vestur, much impressed.

"Yes indeed, she did," said Septabliss. "She told Allusin that she was transforming the worm into a dragon to protect the city, and in the future the dragon will speak to Allusin only. Oh, I forgot, she mentioned another thing. She said the dragon should not be seen by anyone unless the dragon so wishes. That was her dream."

"What an amazing dream!" the high priest said breathlessly. As he knew that Septabliss was illiterate and had never received any religious education or training, Vestur concluded that what Septabliss had said must be the truth.

"I always considered Allusin to be a very special person," said Vestur, "pure and innocent with a big heart to love and to forgive. But I never imagined our Lady would appear and speak to her so explicitly. I would like very much to talk to Allusin herself."

"Was that beautiful woman the Mother Goddess?" asked Septabliss, pretending not to know.

"Yes, the accurate description leaves no room for doubt. But I need to talk to Allusin myself about this," said Vestur firmly.

"Does her dream have any significance?" asked Septabliss.

"Yes, Septabliss. It does. When can I see Allusin?" asked Vestur, impatiently.

"You know how much she loves you and enjoys your teachings at the temple," said Septabliss, "but under this particular circumstance, do you deem it advisable that she leave the dragon alone? Can we be sure that in her absence no one will attempt to enter the room, thus disobeying our Lady's command? Might the dragon be angry?"

"You have a point there. I shall come and visit Allusin myself," said Vestur.

"You are welcome any day you like," said Septabliss. "Allusin will be honored if you pay her a visit. But if we deny the community another day of visitation without giving them a reason, we might create frenzy among the people, and there will be a riot in town. Today we asked the visitors to come back tomorrow, because Allusin was not feeling well and in her absence no one is allowed to approach the dragon. But I cannot come up with the same excuse for the next day. You should see the long lines in front of my house. Every day the old and the ailing are brought in carriages to be healed by the dragon.

Only a formal proclamation from you will convince them. And that must be sent out instantly to prevent any disturbing events from happening. I am sure you agree that it is not wise to deceive or disappoint people, especially those who are desperately in need of help. But, I leave it up to you."

Vestur, convinced of Septabliss's sincerity, assured him that he would send out such a proclamation immediately.

"By the way, have you noticed any changes in the worm lately? You referred to the worm as a dragon?" asked Vestur, as Septabliss was leaving.

"After Allusin described her dream," Septabliss replied, "I did not go to visit the worm as I usually do. I said to myself I had to check with you first to make sure whether or not I should do so. But she did mention that the skin was turning into a bright shining gold and the worm had already grown a tail with four short legs."

"Well then, we know what to do," said Vestur.

When Septabliss returned home he told Allusin that the high priest also believed the change to be a holy event and he was going to issue a proclamation right away.

"You see, my dear daughter, it is exactly as I told you. We are blessed with a holy dragon."

"But it has no legs and no tail," protested Allusin.

"We do not interfere with heaven's description of a dragon. Surely it is a special kind of dragon. Not all dragons bring fortune to people, do they? But this one does, does it not?"

"You are right, Father. It is a special kind of dragon. Maybe later it will become a proper dragon," a disheartened Allusin said.

That afternoon Vestur sent out this proclamation to be read to people in the four squares located in the four corners of the town:

> Let it be known to all the people of Kolallan that it was the wishes of our Lady to transform the worm into a golden dragon to protect our city. It is also her wish that no one should attempt to visit the sacred dragon until he receives

direct orders from me. Insubordination will be severely punished. You may take your offerings to the house of Septabliss as usual, and they will be taken to the sacred dragon. No blessings will be missed by not visiting him in person.

The next day Septabliss went to see the high priest again and said that the dragon had spoken to Allusin.

"What did the dragon say?" Vestur asked.

"The dragon wishes a citadel built for him," said Septabliss.

"A citadel?" the high priest repeated. "What in heaven's name for?"

"A citadel with seven towers, colored black, white, purple, red, blue, green, and yellow," said Septabliss quickly.

It became quite obvious to Vestur that Septabliss had memorized it all. He regretted his proclamation, realizing that he had fallen into a trap from which it would be difficult to free himself. For the time being it was almost impossible to alter the course of events.

"Interesting! Seven towers! Did he say in which tower he wanted to be located? Perhaps in the yellow one in the middle?" said Vestur.

"Exactly! How did you guess?" asked Septabliss.

"It is my duty to know," he replied coldly.

Noticing Vestur's discomfort, Septabliss said harshly, "The whole vitality of the town and the people depends on fulfilling the dragon's wishes. We all lose if the dragon becomes angry."

Vestur turned his head, showing his lack of interest in the subject.

"By the way, the dragon has asked to be called Bouriaz," said Septabliss.

"A curious name! But if that is the chosen name, he should be called by that," said the high priest.

Septabliss was about to leave when Vestur asked him, "How did the dragon speak with Allusin?"

Septabliss confidently replied that Allusin said it happened at dawn. She felt somehow cold and was not sure whether she was dreaming or awake when she heard a deep voice that was warm and kind. Afterwards she fell into a deep sleep. But when she awoke she clearly remembered every word that had been spoken.

Septabliss left the hall with a victorious smile on his face. He held his head up and straightened his back. He walked like a conqueror pleased with himself and the world.

Vestur was disturbed by Septabliss's confident reply. At that point he was certain that Septabliss had enlisted the help of a priest in his elaborate plot. Knowing all the others well, Vestur concluded that the coconspirator must be Amaease. Heartbroken, he went to the altar to pray:

"Oh heavenly queen! Forgive me for failing to see the deception that will bring great harm to this city and its people. I beg of you to give me a chance to prove my worth to heaven and give me the strength to combat this rising evil. Septabliss and Amaease will ruin the good life that you graciously have bestowed upon us!"

For the rest of the day and throughout the night Vestur refused food and drink and stood in front of the altar chanting hymns and pleading for forgiveness in a trembling voice.

Amaease, who had been eavesdropping, seized the opportunity to make sure that other priests at the temple saw Vestur in that agonized and distressful state of mind. The next morning he poisoned Vestur's milk. Before Vestur could talk to Allusin, he drank the milk at breakfast and had what appeared to be a stroke, becoming completely paralyzed.

Since Amaease's medicinal knowledge was assumed to be superior to all, he took charge of Vestur's healing process. He carefully misguided the priests who were tending to Vestur, thus causing Vestur's death within two weeks.

Amaease explained to everyone that Vestur had died of deep spiritual injuries to his heart. Since oracles were always conveyed to the people through the high priest's visions or dreams, Vestur regarded Allusin's prophetic dreams as personal humiliation. He believed that he had failed to follow heavenly orders, and that was the reason the Mother

Goddess had stripped him of his spiritual authority by choosing Allusin and the dragon to be the medium for her heavenly messages.

Septabliss, accepting Amaease's explanation for Vestur's death, was relieved. Septabliss believed that his lies were justified in the eyes of heaven because they had removed Vestur and not him. Now he totally trusted Amaease, since he was the one who had predicted that Vestur would surely collapse under pressure of losing his spiritual authority.

On Septabliss's strong recommendation, Amaease became the high priest.

In his new position, Amaease was commissioned by Septabliss to send a search crew to find the best architects, stonecutters, painters, sculptors, artists, and even magicians. Amaease was well aware of the fact that he needed a specific system in order for his project to succeed. Thus, he designed a precise format for himself and began to follow it step by step. He met with each craftsman separately, promising money, land, and high positions according to their particular needs and backgrounds, of which he had gained complete knowledge before the meetings. Then he announced that on Tuesday, the twenty-first of the month, which was an auspicious day to begin a successful project, there would be a meeting in Septabliss's house.

On that day, after a large feast, Amaease, with Septabliss at his side, gave a speech.

"You were all carefully chosen for your talents, for your integrity, and for your devotion to this land. We firmly believe in these qualities. Our divine Lady has ordered us to build a fortress for our gracious dragon, Bouriaz. She has been very specific in her plans for this fortress, revealing the details to our benefactor Septabliss's daughter, Allusin, through the dragon. Since we will be dealing with hundreds and hundreds of laborers, many of them of foreign origin, whoever works on this project has to take a pledge of secrecy upon his honor and life not to discuss the details of the plan with anyone outside the domain of his work.

"The project will be handled in a pyramid of information and coordination. The lower base does not have access to activities above its rank but bears responsibility for the ones below. There will be a council consisting of all the professionals on top who are responsible and answerable to Septabliss and myself. So, each of you is expected to keep our progress secret unless otherwise advised.

"All of you will be well provided for during construction. Food and shelter will be given to anyone who asks. Your family will be taken care of, and any supplies or materials you need will be delivered. However, any mistakes will be regarded as serious, and negligence will not be tolerated. For your diligence and discretion you will be rewarded. Anyone who does not submit to these conditions is free to leave now. But for those of you who are courageous enough to stay, you will have signed a sacred pact with Heaven. This pact is an agreement to obey the wishes of your superiors and to protect this project with your lives.

"Now we will leave this chamber for one hour to give you enough time to discuss the matter amongst yourselves and to give you a chance to leave if you so decide."

When they returned an hour later, only one person was missing. No one could remember his face, although some described him as a figure with white hair wearing a blue mantel. Septabliss looked at Amaease with inquiring eyes, but Amaease only shrugged his shoulders and addressed the gathering:

"We are so proud! Today you have exhibited your courage and dedication to our land and to our divinities. It is the wish of our Lady and the command of our dragon Bouriaz that this fortress be finished within one year, six months, twenty-five days, and seventeen hours, starting the first day of the next month. It is my holy duty to supervise the project day and night to make sure that it is finished during this period. I warn you that unless the fortress is occupied by our holy dragon by the appointed time, cataclysmic events undoubtedly will follow. The angry dragon will swallow the sun and the moon, and darkness will fall!"

5

Thousands of slaves were brought in, and hundreds of skilled laborers hired to work around the clock to finish the fortress by the appointed date.

During the construction, Amaease spent most of his time at the site, talking to everyone, inspecting everything, and ordering the laborers around, rewarding and punishing them according to their progress or mistakes. He made most of the occupants of the orphanage and the poorhouse work at the site without pay. At the same time, he cheated Septabliss on the expenditures and pocketed money from all the transactions made. He gradually began to form an army and cautiously chose the officers on whose loyalty he could count. Amaease consulted Septabliss on trivial matters to gratify his fragile confidence but did not involve Septabliss in the important issues. Septabliss was pleased that Amaease had taken charge of the project and did not bother him with the details.

By the time construction was completed the worm had turned into a three-headed terrifying creature, as big as an elephant, whose loud occasional shrieks could be heard from miles away.

The fortress was built on thousands of acres at the shores of Lake Yent. Two streams flowed out of this lake in opposite directions. The water level never changed during the seasons, so people believed Lake Yent to be sacred. Around the fortress three fortification walls were built, each 450 feet tall and sixteen feet deep. The two outermost walls, between which there was a narrow passage spanning the lake and the land, had 107 watchtowers. The outside wall had only one entrance, which faced south. A bridge over a deep moat filled with water connected the gate to the rest of the town. The innermost wall, which was square, surrounded the main building with thirty-two watchtowers and had two entrances. There was an adjacent building connected to the towers by underground tunnels. It was here that Septabliss kept his office. An eighteen-room guesthouse was built next to that office. There were large stables for the best horses, which were used for chariots, cavalry, and pages. There was also a big ice-house at the eastern wing of the fortress, to keep the milk fresh during hot summer days.

The inner fortification wall, which protected the main building, consisted of seven separate towers. Six were arranged in a circle. Though they differed in height, because of their locations on the slopes of a stony hill, from afar they appeared to be the same height. The only exception was the tower in the middle, which was the tallest and had a high dome. All the towers were connected with covered corridors on the surface and contained underground passages with secret doors.

One heptagon tower was seven stories high, with seven columns at each corner, and was covered with inlaid black agate stone. The interior walls were decorated with lead motifs of goatfish and a man sitting on a stool, under which was the image of a large fish. This tower was for infantry, with hammers of steel and with clubs cast out of strong red brass. The insignia of a standing dragon with upward wings on the armor was in black. There were seven guards on duty around the clock in this watchtower.

One triangular tower, six stories high, with three columns on each corner, was for charioteers. The columns were covered with amethysts. The interior walls were decorated with tin motifs of mermaids and archers and centurions on the move. The insignia of a dragon with outstretched wings on the armor was in purple. There were three guards on duty around the clock in this watchtower.

One oblong tower, five stories high, had four columns on each corner and was covered with inlaid bloodstone. The interior walls were decorated with iron motifs of a tall bearded man with an armband carrying a staff and large scorpions in different positions. This quarter was assigned to the special guards with long iron spears, well whetted and sharp. The insignia of two dragons standing back-to-back on the armor was in red. There were eight guards on duty day and night in this watchtower.

One square tower, three stories high, had three columns around its center forming a triangle. The columns were inlaid with white alabaster. The interior walls were decorated with copper motifs of cone-shaped scales and a charioteer driving a bull. In this tower lived the dragon's servants: beautiful girls below the age of fourteen who were trained to sing, dance, and play the lute. Adorned with garlands of fresh flowers on their heads, they formed a procession each morning and evening. As they walked they carried milk in golden buckets and honey in golden bowls, chanting:

O celestial dragon Bouriaz!
The wealth bestowing, comfort providing!
From miseries of poverty, safeguarding.
Milk of a thousand cows we offer thee!
Honey of ten thousand bees we offer thee!
At sunrise and at sunset
Focused on your graciousness,
With hearts grateful and happy,
Humbly your blessings we seek!

They would leave the bowls and the buckets at the entrance hall for Allusin to take to the dragon. They wore white cotton tunics and long wraparound white skirts with short white silk vests. The insignia of a reclining dragon was woven in gold silk on their vests, with the dragon's head on the shoulder and its tail spiraling down. There were five guards day and night in this watchtower.

One two-story oblong tower had three columns around its center forming a triangle. The columns were covered with inlaid tourmaline, and the interior walls were decorated with iron motifs of a lady sitting on a dolphin, carrying a palm leaf in her left hand and the tail of a snake in her right. There were motifs of two maidens sitting on a bench side-by-side looking at each other. This tower was assigned to archers with falcon-feathered arrows. The insignia on their armor of a flying dragon with outstretched wings was in blue. There were nine guards day and night in this watchtower.

One octagon tower, one story high, had eight columns on each corner and was covered with inlaid moonstone. The interior walls were decorated with silver crescent moons and full moons. This tower was assigned to the swift cavalry. The insignia of a seated dragon with wings thrown back was stamped on their armors in green. There were eight guards day and night in this watchtower.

In the center of the circle was the golden dragon's tower, square in shape, with a column at each corner. Unlike the others, this tower had a domed ceiling. Twelve men in golden armor guarded the tower from sunrise to sunset, and twelve from night until dawn. Though this tower was only four stories high it was taller than the rest. It had mirrored walls; its mirrored floor moved very slowly counterclockwise and on it lay a pure golden statue of a dragon with its wings closed and its feet hidden under its body. On its domed ceiling, which moved clockwise and faster than the floor, the major constellations were painted. There was no access to this hall other than one peephole in the south wall, which people called the "Kot of the dragon." When seen through that hole the dragon's head was above the center and his body encircled the constellation of the Little Bear.

Adjacent to the mirrored hall was the home of the three-headed worm with no wings and no tail. The worm's hall was actually a large wide tunnel of black marble with no external windows. It had one connecting door to Allusin's living room. Allusin had one bedroom and one living room which both were luxuriously furnished in a style fit for a princess. Each one had large windows facing the north. Her bedroom door opened to a narrow passage which led to the entrance, where two men stood guard at all times. The servants provided her with whatever she needed, however, no one was allowed to enter her quarters.

Gigantic storage facilities were built and filled with a three-year supply of wheat, rice, millet, and wood. Huge square wooden boxes stored imported cinnamon, three different kinds of musk from China, and turmeric from India. Large treasure rooms were piled high with gold, silver, pearls, silk, wool, cotton, and furs. There were offices for the accountants, scribes, and counselors who ran the business of the fortress and the city of Kolallan.

6

wo nights before the opening ceremony, when there was no moon in the sky, the worm was transported to the fortress in an enormous box completely covered by a black blanket. Amaease himself carefully chose the architect, the artist, and the few laborers involved in the construction of the golden dragon's mirrored hall. They were foreigners, with no family ties in the city, and they departed before the worm was transported to the fortress. The rumor was that they were suddenly summoned by the king and had to leave before the celebration day.

The night before their departure Amaease had invited them over to have dinner with him and receive handsome rewards for the job they had done so well. It was the fourth time during the past eighteen months that he had done so. On each occasion, which was a religious celebration, he ordered wine to be served to all, including the servants of the temple. This time was no different. Everyone knew from the beginning of the project about the one special wine barrel that was reserved to celebrate the end of the construction. So they all antici- pated tasting that particular wine. As the wine was mixed with a sleeping potion, it put everyone into a deep sleep for several hours. When the servants awoke, Amaease scorned them for drinking too much and for their sloppy service of the night, of which no one had any recollection. There was also no witness to the guests' departure.

During the construction of the fortress, Amaease had made several additions to the temple. One was a large receiving hall. It was built with one secret door, behind which was an underground passage. The next addition was a bedroom with another secret door leading to a storage area, where he kept his treasures. The secret storage had a long underground passage to the stable area. At the far end of the receiving hall, underneath his personal altar, where he pretended to pray every day, a deep ditch was dug. Its entrance was blocked by a large piece of marble, which was always covered by a heavy rug. Amaease single-handedly dumped his guests' bodies into the ditch, poured nitric acid on them, and closed its entrance. He kept the gold coins that Septabliss had intended for his guests

People assumed that Allusin was the happiest maiden in Kolallan because she had the blessing to be at the site of the dragon at all times and was the sole person chosen to feed him. From the day the worm changed, Allusin had noticed that everybody around her was behaving strangely and that fewer and fewer people spent time with her. Even her mother rarely visited her. The only two people she saw every day were her father and Pearl, a Zanzibarian slave, who told her that Allusin was not allowed to receive the news of the outside world. After Vestur's death she had no desire to go back to the temple anyhow. She accepted her fate with the hope that soon after the prince returned, everything would change.

One week before the big move, Visseh went to say farewell to her daughter.

"Mother," said Allusin, "am I going to be in that tower all by myself with this creature? Will Pearl stay with me or not?"

Visseh's response was one of outrage: "How dare you call our divine dragon a creature? This is a wicked thing to say! You are an ungrateful soul, never appreciating the things that are done for you. Doeshat was so jealous of you when she heard about your splendid rooms in the golden tower. For your own sake I am not going to tell your father of this nonsensical complaint, lest in his anger he should send Saiparak away. You know that he never liked this stupid dog."

"If Saiparak is taken away, I will not feed the worm anymore, and the worm will die. Every day when I come back from that stinky room, I feel so tired."

"Cleaning one room and taking buckets of milk to the dragon's chamber now makes you tired? Have you already forgotten how hard I had to work every day just to keep your father and your brother happy? It is sacrilegious to be disrespectful towards the divine power, which has made us all so rich. Do not call the holy dragon a worm! It may bring us bad luck."

"I do not want that luxury. I do not enjoy that kind of comfort. I want my freedom back, and I do not care what you call it!" said Allusin. "It is a worm to me. The reason for my patience is because I know that I am not going to be in that tower for long."

"What do you mean, Allusin? What are you going to do? Where are you going to go?" asked Visseh.

"I do not know yet. I need more time to think about it. I must wait a little longer," replied Allusin sadly.

Allusin had to force herself to go to the worm's chamber to pour food into its mouths. Keeping the lie a secret was also a heavy burden on her heart. Many times she decided to run away, but each time when she thought of the thriving town and her happily married friends, she changed her mind. She feared that without her, misery might befall her family and the people of Kolallan.

Visseh told her husband about the conversation she had with Allusin. Septabliss immediately sent for Amaease and passed the information to him.

"When Vestur was alive," said Amaease, "one day your daughter went to the temple. I happened to be nearby and overheard her. I remember that she asked Vestur about the advancement of the war and whether or not he had any news from the prince. A strange subject to interest a girl, I thought. I also recall that some time ago you told me that she refused to marry anyone, did you not, Septabliss?"

Septabliss nodded, and Amaease continued, "It seems that the prince has promised something to your daughter. Perhaps she is waiting for him. She must be stupid to believe that the prince would marry a commoner, but nevertheless, this is what I suggest. Before we move the dragon to the tower let us tell your daughter that the prince was killed in battle. When she is isolated in the tower there will be no way for her to find out the truth. That is if you can make sure that she does not contact anyone. You can at least manage a simple thing like that, can you not?"

"Simple it is," said Septabliss, "but I do not wish her to fall ill. Her life is valuable to us. She seems to be losing weight. Besides, what should we tell the prince when he comes back?"

"First of all, nothing is going to happen to her," said Amaease. "She will weep a little, mourn a little, and then she will forget. Trust me, all women are like that. Their hearts do not mourn for long, though they pretend otherwise. I will prepare something for her to boost her vitality. And as for the prince, you simply tell him that Allusin decided to dedicate her life to her beloved dragon. Since that is her wish he must respect it. We just do not want to injure his young pride. He knows that many maidens devote their lives to the temple and the order of the priesthood. We have four of them there. I have no doubt that there are quite a few good-looking maidens of royal background waiting for him. I do not believe there was a big bond between the prince and Allusin. We will give her the news next week before the big move. She will be slightly sedated for one week so she can perform her duties and remain emotionally calm. I know how to handle my part, and I hope you will do your side as flawlessly as I have done mine. I will not have to see this town be ruined because of a maiden who is not even of noble birth. Agreed?"

"Yes, of course! I also remember something else that Allusin told me, concerning the ring that Peerbabu gave her."

"What ring?" asked Amaease, surprised. "Why have you never told me about it?"

"It is just a ruby ring that she wears. I never thought it had any significance," said Septabliss.

"What do you know about the significance of anything? What exactly did she say?" asked Amaease.

"That no one else should wear that ring except her," Septabliss said.

"Did you ask her why?" asked Amaease impatiently.

"I did ask her, but she said that Peerbabu never explained."

"Maybe it is because of this ring that only she can feed the dragon?" said Amaease, as if he had struck gold.

Whenever Amaease failed to reach a conclusion by rationalizing, he considered the event supernatural. He believed that human beings were able to control and manipulate supernatural powers. He had searched many libraries and studied hundreds of ancient books and manuscripts, looking for clues to gain such magical power. To him the worm was the source of wealth and power, but he could not quite figure out the connection between Allusin and the worm. So, he had resigned himself to the idea that for the time being Allusin's function was essential to the progress of his project, as was Septabliss's position, although Septabliss had become more of a nuisance than help. Possessing the ring could dramatically alter the course of events.

"Who knows," continued Amaease, concealing his glee, "since you are Allusin's father, maybe with the ring you too can feed the dragon! You are the blessed Septabliss, are you not? We must find the answer. This puts you in a position of control, not falling hostage to the moods of a naïve maiden. When she becomes irrelevant you are free to do as you wish, and she could marry whomever she wants! You must remove the ring while she is put to sleep and make an attempt to feed the dragon. If it works, then you will become the master. But for your own sake, your son should never find this out. You were unwise to put him in command of the army. History is filled with stories of sons turning against their fathers to gain access to their thrones and treasures."

Septabliss agreed that it was a brilliant idea.

However, when Amaease left, Septabliss had conflicting emotions.

He was pleased with Amaease's suggestions and warnings but was bitter about his humiliating attitude. Septabliss began to fear Amaease's power. Nervously he paced the room.

"This hideous priest is becoming too haughty. Now he dares to order me around. He was just a miser priest. I made him the high priest. If I decide not to support him anymore, he will become powerless. He is nobody. On the other hand, his help is still crucial to me. Maybe the ring will bring me the strength to overpower him. Perhaps from the very beginning the ring was meant to be mine, but I do not want to be in charge of the feeding. It is a big commitment and a menial task. Perhaps by the power of the ring I can manage the worm's feeding to be done by someone else. Amaease was right about Vantu. I must watch my son. Doeshat has great influence on him and could provoke him to plot against me. She is sneaky and unappreciative. The more I give them, the more she demands. In that pigeon mind of hers she does not see that Vantu is merely a figurehead in this organization. Even a fool knows that a drunk who sleeps until noon is incapable of leading a large army. If it were not for the shrewd commanders whom Amaease has hired, we would not have a disciplined army."

Allusin's first reaction to the news of the prince's death was devastation. She fainted and remained lifeless for hours. There was no need to give her the potion that Amaease had concocted.

The moment Septabliss removed the ring from Allusin's finger Saiparak became violent and wildly attacked him. He had to fight his way out of the room and was bleeding all over. Saiparak did not follow him but stayed at Allusin's side. Septabliss sent for his physician, who cleaned and bandaged his wounds.

"That evil dog will not see the light of another day," shouted Septabliss. "He has been nothing but trouble for us since he was brought to my house. I swear I will have him burned alive tonight!"

He rested awhile, and when it was time to feed the worm, he went to the entrance to the worm's quarters. There he found the three pots of milk and honey, which he carried inside. He locked the door. He was nervous. He had avoided visiting the worm since it had developed two more heads. His eyes popped out in terror. Unable to avert his gaze, he gasped for air when he saw the gigantic body of the worm. The worm was staring at him. Septabliss saw himself in the creature's eyes as if looking into six convex mirrors. He saw three blazing beams converging in the center, and then like an arrow they pierced his navel. They cut through his stomach and traveled up his spine, dispersing in his head and his limbs. His skin began to itch and tighten as if it were cracking. A sudden thirst dried his throat and a cramp blasted his stomach. He felt as if he were drowning in the worm's red eyes. Septabliss could no longer tell the difference between himself and the worm—at that moment he was not sure whether he was in the worm or the worm was in him. The worm's anger was as real to him as his own fear.

The worm crunched its body. A threatening shriek echoed in the empty hall. Septabliss's reaction was to flee for survival. He turned around and threw himself out, then fell down behind the door.

Standing there was Allusin with Saiparak at her side. She was pale, hurt, and disgusted. Without a word she took the ring from her fallen father's finger and left. As she put it on, she noticed that the color was almost black! The prince was dead. Tears streamed down her face as she fainted again.

The worm began to shriek. It was time for feeding.

Septabliss sent for Amaease.

"The ring is useless in anyone else's hand. Your knowledge is worthless. You pretend to know everything. But you are only a petty priest who cannot perform even simple magic. See what you have done!" Septabliss said. "Can you not hear how the dragon is shrieking? It is your fault! You made me do it. Who is going to feed the dragon while Allusin remains unconscious? People will panic if he continues to make such threatening noises. What are we going to do?"

Amaease ignored Septabliss's insult. He was not offended by the one whom he considered to be "a little man." He offered Septabliss a spoonful of a tonic he had brought with him, but Septabliss refused.

"How am I to trust you? How should I know that you want to

help me and not kill me? I have had nothing but trouble since you came to this town. What did we need a fortress for? What did we need an army for? These problems are the result of your useless mind."

"My knowledge is not worthless, and my mind is not useless," replied Amaease calmly "You are of no use to me dead, and neither is your daughter. I would not benefit from killing either of you. The worm is only demanding to be fed, but eventually it will slow down and fall asleep. Now drink this and stop the nonsense. Take my word that you are safe with me! If I were you I would try to produce more children. If Allusin was blessed with this ring, how do you know that the others would not be? You are still young. With more daughters like Allusin, you need not worry about a thing as long as you live. What do you have to lose by trying it?"

These words had immediate effect on Septabliss. He was amused by the suggestion, for it gave him a legitimate reason to make his adulterous behavior public. He drank the tonic and soon felt better. The worm stopped shrieking. Once again doubts about Amaease were erased from Septabliss's mind.

"I am going to stay with Allusin tonight," said Amaease. "This potion should be given to her on time without interruption."

"But you cannot do that. Saiparak will not let you stay there."

"The dog that Peerbabu gave her?"

"Yes."

"Who is staying with her now?"

"Pearl."

"Animals understand when someone comes to help. I want to see his reaction for myself. The dosage and the time are crucial with this medicine," insisted Amaease.

As he approached her room, he heard the dog's bark. When he opened the door, Saiparak was right behind it. He began to growl like a lioness protecting her cubs, poised to attack. He looked vicious and unrelenting. Amaease was struck with fear that was an unfamiliar sensation to him. He realized that he could not overcome the power he was confronting and had to withdraw.

"He is not an ordinary dog. As long as he is around no one can harm her. Why does Peerbabu protect Allusin? Is the worm his creation? What does he get out of it? I wish I could see this weird old man. What people say about him is garbage. Surely he knows the art of magic, and at times is lucky enough to make things happen, but it is idiotic to believe that he can talk to birds and animals. Someday I shall solve this puzzle."

Pearl stayed at Allusin's bedside and gradually gave her the potion throughout the night. Early in the morning Allusin opened her eyes and glanced at her ring. The color was bright red! She remembered the events of the day before and smiled. She knew that the prince was still alive. She had regained her strength and felt energetic. Seeing his daughter healthy again, Septabliss felt that he had misjudged Amaease. He apologized for the things he had said and began to trust Amaease again.

A big feast planned for Saturday, the sixteenth day of the first month of autumn. High-ranking people with their families gathered in a large mirrored hall on the ground floor of the golden tower. The rest of the town's people waited outside to enter the fortress later. Septabliss, who was clothed like a male peacock and was lost in his own imaginary grandeur, addressed the gathering:

"My honored guests! The glorious dragon Bouriaz, who has delivered this town from misery and despair, has blessed us with his presence in the golden tower. His growth has become our growth. He has made us rich in offspring and monetary wealth. Now I ask our revered High Priest Amaease to lead us in prayer."

Amaease, who had dressed equally magnificently, raised his hands:

O gracious dragon Bouriaz,
The light of paradise!
You blessed us with a thousand females of all species.
You blessed our pastures with oxen many!
You blessed our fields with horses many!

We beg of you:
Drive away all manner of sickness!
Drive away all manner of pain!
Take away the strength from our enemy!
Take away swiftness from the feet of our enemy!
Take away eyesight from the eyes of our enemy!
Take away the hearing from the ears of our enemy!
You are the victory making!
You are the army governing!
You are the power possessing,
Endowed with a thousand senses!
Bless us with the fair blessing spells of the dragon!

Amaease, proud and impressed with his own performance, continued:

"Chosen people of Kolallan, it is the wish of the gracious dragon that you make your offerings generous and swift so that you make room for others to enter and pay their respects as well."

The horns sounded and people cheered outside. Everybody stood in line for hours with gold ornaments, fresh flower garlands, and milk and honey awaiting their turn to peep through the Kot of the dragon Bouriaz. All the priests and their apprentices were at hand and were well prepared to provide convincing answers to their questions.

"How come we never see the dragon fly?"

The answer was: "He flies in the shape of a raven. He flies in the shape of a horse. But only pure eyes can see him fly as a dragon."

"Where does he fly?"

And they were told: "This dragon is from the heavenly race. He flies to heaven. Constellation Draco is his heavenly abode."

"Does he breathe fire?"

"Only when he is angry."

"What makes him angry?"

"The profanity of ungrateful people."

The celebration continued for seven days and seven nights. Torches were lit in all the watchtowers and were kept burning from dusk until dawn. Bouquets of aromatic plants covered the surface of the lake. Garlands of flowers decorated the towers according to their colors.

Unlike the old festivities in town prior to the appearance of the worm, this public celebration was divided. The wealthy and the prominent did not mingle with the rest. Their homes were decorated with scented flowers, palm leaves, and spruce. Inside, large wooden tables with legs carved in the shape of animal heads were laid with large silver platters of meat and beans. Foods were cooked not on fire made of wood, but on plants and grass, as was the custom in religious festivities. Soups made with different herbs, beans, and sheep's milk filled large bowls. Plates were filled with pistachios, walnuts, figs, almonds, dates, peaches, and raisins. There were loaves of bread cooked with wheat flour, sugar, sheep's milk, and turmeric. Children were served the juice of fruits cooked in sugar, and adults enjoyed endless cups of wine.

The rest of the town's people, in large groups, shared simple meals and sang and danced in the squares till dawn.

<h1 style="text-align:center">7</h1>

 llusin's sole companion while confined to the dragon's quarters was Saiparak. Each day she stood by the window and prayed to the spirit of the rising sun:

O glorious lord of nations!
The kind keeper of creation,
Your abode high and bright is far and wide.
There comes neither night nor darkness.
O lord of pastures wide!
With a thousand ears hearing,
Fully awake!
With ten thousand eyes watching.
Strong you are and sleepless.
O beneficent Lord!
My good valiant prince I no longer see.
My heart in distress is grieving.
May the voice of my wailing reach your dwelling!
You worthy of praise! I humbly beg:
Deliver me from the dragon fortress!
Grant me joy! Grant me happiness!

She was miserable and becoming frailer as days went by. To make her lonesome hours pass faster, from the day she transferred to the tower she began to weave ropes. As if it were the length of the ropes that gave her the strength and hope she needed to survive.

One night as she was watching the stars she thought of Peerbabu.

"Peerbabu," said she, "you must have forgotten me, too. But I understand you cannot enter this fortress, let alone come to my quarters. I had promised my father that I would never reveal the secret of the worm, but I guess he never believed me. I am so grateful that you gave me Saiparak. If it were not for the hope of my prince returning to me and the companionship of Saiparak, I would have perished."

All of a sudden, Peerbabu appeared!

"Peerbabu!" she cried with joy. "How did you get here?"

"Old people find ways to get around. You look a little pale, Allusin. Are you eating well?" asked Peerbabu.

Allusin told him that, although she looked at her ring every day and was sure that nothing had happened to the prince, sometimes she could not help feeling sad, abandoned, and forgotten. Other times she did not feel anything at all, as if her life were on hold. Peerbabu assured her that the prince was alive and well and would arrive the following week. As they were talking, the worm began to move toward Allusin's chamber and shrieked in an unusual way. Allusin threw herself at Peerbabu and grabbed his garment. Saiparak dashed to the door and ferociously barked at the worm.

"Do not let this creature frighten you!" said Peerbabu, comforting her. "It can smell my presence. Saiparak knows how to handle him. I shall be back soon with more good news. You must promise that you will never yield to despair. It will not be long before you will be united with the prince, but you need to keep your spirits up. I see you are weaving ropes. When did you start doing this?"

"Since they put me in this tower. This tower is so high, and I am so far away from people and my favorite hills. I cannot smell the fresh grass or touch the cool water of the springs. Weaving ropes makes me feel better, as if I could do those things when they get long enough to reach the ground. It sounds silly, does it not, Peerbabu?"

"No, it is not, my dear child. Your heart knows where to lead you, and you are pure enough to follow it. People's hearts often talk but not many listen. In due time we shall make good use of them. You keep weaving, the longer the better. And I want you to do something else. I would like you to put one drop of this liquid in the worm's milk every time you feed it. But be very careful about the dosage. Not more than a drop, Allusin!"

"Do not worry, Peerbabu. I will do as I am told."

Peerbabu said, "Then I bid you farewell, and will see you soon, Allusin." And he whispered to the dog, "Your performance is impeccable, Saiparak!" With that he disappeared into the dark.

8

he triumphant and anxious prince returned home. He had received the highest badge of bravery. Barzin greeted him outside the prince's castle. His first question for Barzin was about Allusin.

"I have heard several stories about how Kolallan has changed," said the prince. "I heard about a fortress being built there, and about Septabliss. But have you any news from Allusin?"

"People say that she is in the tower with the dragon," said Barzin, "but nothing is certain. There is a high wall of secrecy around the whole thing. No one talks. Some visiting the town told me that she feeds the dragon that made her weave fast. That is all I know."

"What dragon?" asked the stunned prince, "The day before my departure Allusin told me that she had found a worm, and the worm made her weave faster. But what is this dragon, and from where did it come?"

"It is a strange kind of dragon, so the rumors say," replied Barzin. "It was a worm, but magically, by the wish of our Mother Goddess, became a dragon. Now he is the one whom the people of Kolallan worship."

"It is sheer nonsense," said the prince, "A worm does not grow to become a dragon. Even by magic it cannot stay a dragon forever. Dragons are born as dragons."

"There are curious stories about the citadel and the dragon," Barzin said. "But no one knows the truth. Or perhaps those who do never talk."

"I am going to see Uncle Sarabaress," said the prince. And without even entering his own castle, he rode straight to his uncle's home.

Prince Sarabaress greeted the prince heartily.

"Welcome, my son! There is not a happier soul than me today. Divinities have saved you to save this land, and you have proven to be worthy of it. The news of your heroic deeds has reached us. You have already become a legend."

"Uncle Sarabaress! I am happy to find you in good health," said the prince. "My heroic deeds, I should admit, have not much to do with myself, but to the love that made me feel invincible."

"Who is this lucky girl? Do I know her? Where did you meet her?" asked Sarabaress.

"She is the daughter of Adaddera," said the prince, "I learned that nowadays people call him Septabliss."

"Septabliss of Kolallan?" asked Sarabaress, even more surprised.

"Yes. I knew her before I went to war and promised her marriage upon my return," said the prince.

"Did you give her the jade pendant?"

"Yes I did. When I met her I was so overwhelmed by my own feelings that I was not certain what I wanted to do. But when the departure day approached I realized how much she meant to me. So I gave her the pendant. I should have told you about her earlier, but I never got a chance to see you in private."

"In that case, I will dispatch someone to go to Kolallan and gather useful information for us. Then we shall proceed accordingly," said Sarabaress.

"I do not want to be disobedient, uncle, but I cannot wait even one more day. I do not know why, but I fear for her life. I heard that she is in a tower and feeds a dragon. I know her very well. She surrenders to compassion like a sacrificial lamb. I want to make sure that she is not in any danger."

"But my dear son, do you not think you are being too hasty? Why should she be in danger?"

"I have no explanation to offer. I do not expect anyone to understand it. Sometimes I do not understand it myself. I can only tell you that in the war I did not fight for glory, and now my accomplishments mean nothing if I lose her in life. When I was badly wounded, only the thought of her brought me back from death. She has become my source of enduring strength, my hope, my dream, and my future. The badge of bravery I received from the king is the manifestation of my love for her."

"Believe me! I do see your torrential emotions and the restlessness in you. Septabliss's position does not require this courtesy, but in my view it is more appropriate for me to handle this matter. Besides, to honor a maiden, traditionally it is proper that I, as the senior member of the family, pay a visit to Septabliss, offering the proposal on your behalf. Now that I come to think of it, I have not been to Kolallan for a long time. I have heard that it has changed a great deal. I shall dispatch my page tonight to announce my arrival and I will depart early tomorrow morning. What do you think?"

"I am grateful and truly honored! You must forgive me for compromising your position. I have a feeling, though, that you are not confident about Septabliss's response," said the prince.

"You are very sharp, my prince. I have never met Septabliss, so I cannot yet judge," replied Sarabaress with a fatherly smile. "He must be a clever person, to reach the position he has. I need to see him and decide for myself. Best you go wash, rest, and then join me for dinner. I was planning a big welcoming feast later in the week to celebrate your arrival with family and friends, but I will postpone it until I get back. By then we may have more reasons to celebrate."

After dinner the two talked for a long time.

"King Vima is very much impressed with your performance, you know," said Sarabaress.

"How so?"

"I received a letter from him. Not that I was surprised, but it was sooner than I had expected. He may give you the whole southern region to rule. This is a significant position. Usually this type of position is reserved for the crown prince. But, as you know, his older son was killed in the battle and his younger one died last year as well. That means he is left with no heir. His brother is too old and his nephew is not quite fit for the job."

"Are you saying the king is considering me for the throne?"

"This is exactly what I mean. That is why I am concerned about the whole situation with Septabliss."

"I hope you are not suggesting that I should give her up? Because to me losing her would mean losing my soul!"

"Not at all!" replied Sarabaress quickly. "You must trust me. Your happiness is my main concern. An unhappy heart makes an unhappy ruler whose judgment is clouded and compassion self-serving."

"You are wise with words. I wish I had your wisdom and was not so quick to respond," said the prince.

"You, like your father, have a brilliant mind, which I lack," said Sarabaress in a fatherly tone.

"Since I knew that you and my father were so close, I always thought it was very painful for you to talk about him, I never asked anything, but I do want to learn more about him. "

"The pain shall always be in my heart. But your presence is very compensating. Between us two he was always the decision maker and the leader. Unlike me, he was sociable and vivacious, but controlling. In war he was courageous and selfless. He thought of his soldiers as part of his own family, but he had no tolerance for insubordination and was unforgiving to the point of becoming ruthless. At times, in sports and among women, his competitive nature drove him to jealousy. He welcomed challenging discussions but usually turned them into arguments. He did not accept a defeat gracefully, whether in action or in words. We fought and argued ceaselessly, seeming not to agree on anything, but the underlying truth was that we were not basically very different; we were only striving to complete each other. His loss was a big blow, and it left a void in me. If you had not arrived, I would have lost the desire to continue a normal life. In many ways, especially in your quick reactions to what you disagree with, you remind me of him. His compulsive behavior led to his death. No, he was not wise at heart, I admit. I have not come across many who were."

"Believe me, uncle, Allusin has wisdom of the heart," said the prince. "She is the most generous, forgiving, and yet brave person I have seen. What people do with their senses she does with her heart. She savagely attacks atrocities done to others, yet she forgives the aggressor to the point of endangering her life."

When the prince mentioned Allusin's name Sarabaress's face lit up. Excited, he stood up and embraced the prince.

"Allusin is her name, you said. Of course I believe you, Prince Vallusin!" said Prince Sarabaress, thrilled.

"How come you never called me by this name, uncle?"

"It was spontaneous. Peerbabu had advised us not to until the time came, yet the moment I heard her name my tongue carried yours. So it must be the right time to address you by your real name. You see, my dear Prince Vallusin, names that have profound meanings have a particular echo in the universe. Peerbabu cautioned me not to use it, lest it would bring harm to you. This union brings strength and stability to both of you, and it puts you on the right course in life. It will be very auspicious for our land as well."

Prince Vallusin sat down. For the first time in years all tension left his body. He was happy and pleased that his uncle understood his deep attachment to Allusin and said, "Nothing is more uplifting for a soul than confirmation from a wise man. You have been a good father to me, never denying me anything. I wonder how one develops this kind of wisdom?"

"Only life trained me to be thoughtful, humble, and forgiving. But I am far from being a wise man. I am just experienced. That is all. I wish Peerbabu would have taken me for an apprentice," said Prince Sarabaress.

"What kind of wisdom does Peerbabu have, uncle?"

"He is the breath of wisdom which moves in space. He is the power of good. He is the strength of love. He is the symbol of a triumphant human spirit. He can appear and disappear at his own will, and like the breeze he cannot be contained. But when a soul is imprisoned in the human form, it becomes vulnerable," Sarabaress replied.

"Do you think he would ever consider me an apprentice, uncle?"

"I do not know. He never considered me one."

"What should I do to gain his trust?"

"If I knew I would have done it myself," replied Sarabaress. "It is not up to you to choose your master. The master will choose the seeker when the seeker is ready for the task."

9

The next day Prince Sarabaress went to Kolallan with gifts for Septabliss and offerings to the dragon. He took Barzin with him to keep his company.

Septabliss sent out his battalion of cavaliers on white horses, wearing their splendid uniforms, to escort Prince Sarabaress and his entourage to the fortress. All along the road people were lined up cheering to greet the royal visitor.

The wealth and the glamour of the town greatly stunned Prince Sarabaress. He had never expected the stories to be true. He said to Barzin:

"For a simple peasant, within such a short period of time to become so rich is beyond my wildest imagination. It looks more like a miracle."

"People say it is a miracle," said Barzin. "It is the common belief that whoever brings offerings to the dragon will be rewarded a hundredfold. That is why they are swarming this town. So far it seems to be proving true. Prince Vallusin and I rode many times to this area in the old days, but we never cared to enter the town. There was nothing other than its natural beauty to attract one's eyes. Even the temple looked very modest. What an incredible transformation!"

Prince Sarabaress entered the fortress passing through lines of soldiers who saluted him with their bare dazzling swords. On the towers, horn players announced his arrival by playing a tune, each beginning where the other had finished, in the order of their heights, until he reached the guest quarters. Septabliss and Amaease were standing side by side in magnificent clothes in front of the entrance. Behind them stood six officers carrying flags representing their regiments, and in front of them were twelve handsome young girls in white costumes with garlands of yellow flowers upon their heads. They began to sing in a low voice, creating a vibrant spiritual surrounding.

Septabliss greeted them warmly:

"Welcome, Prince Sarabaress! What an unexpected pleasure! Your presence here is a rare honor. My humble house is not fit to receive royalty. I thought the fortress of the dragon would be more suitable for this occasion. Please come in. What makes you grace us with this visit?"

"The honor is mine, Septabliss. I am here on behalf of my nephew, the good Prince Vallusin, to ask for your daughter's hand in marriage."

Septabliss's warm tone immediately changed.

"Oh I see! I thought you came here to pay homage to the holy Bouriaz. I assumed you have heard about the miracles of our gracious dragon."

"Indeed I have," said Prince Sarabaress. "Your town and this magnificent fortress are the living proof of it. In Prince Vallusin's absence I never found the time to do so. I am sure Prince Vallusin will visit you in due time. I even intend to send the news to the King. A miracle such as this should not be kept local. It is for the higher authorities to spread the message around the country. What I had in mind was to take this opportunity to pay my long overdue respects to your gracious dragon. I have brought trifle offerings for the holy Bouriaz."

Prince Sarabaress's features shocked Amaease. His thin gray hair had soft waves, and his nose was short and pointed like his own father's. But unlike Amaease's father, he did not have the sad downward expression in the corner of his lips, and he walked and talked with complete certainty.

Amaease listened carefully and analyzed every word that Prince Sarabaress was uttering. He was not happy with the way the prince was flattering Septabliss. He knew that Septabliss's great weakness, besides laziness, was the increasing thirst he had to be admired. The idea of sending the message to the King was also alarming to him. From information he had gathered prior to Prince Sarabaress's arrival, the old prince was not the kind of person to believe in miracles such as that. He feared that Septabliss would soon give in to the flattery.

"A wise prince such as you is a rarity nowadays," said Septabliss with a self-satisfied smile. "You are well aware that it was the wish of Our Lady to worship her through the celestial Bouriaz. The blessings will cease if we disobey her wishes."

"Indeed!" confirmed Prince Sarabaress in a low voice.

"Nothing would give me greater pleasure than to fulfill Prince Vallusin's wishes," continued Septabliss, "but you see, my daughter's life is devoted to serving the supreme dragon. The mighty dragon has chosen my daughter to be his sole companion. I am sure you agree that it is the highest blessing and honor for a maiden to be in this position. My daughter—"

Amaease cut him short:

"Prince Sarabaress! As the chief council of the Lady of Immaculate Waters, I ask your permission to reveal the fact that Allusin is not allowed to marry a mortal regardless of his nobility. This is according to the oracles of the temple of our Lady. Allusin no longer lives in our realm. Her spirit moves with the dragon, her heart beats with the dragon. She has the dragon's heart."

Prince Sarabaress immediately realized Amaease's authority and control over Septabliss and the uselessness of further engaging in discussion with them.

"I fully understand your position, Septabliss," said Prince Sarabaress, ignoring the interruption. "I am sure Prince Vallusin will respect Our Lady's wishes as well. Now, may I have the honor of personally presenting the offerings to the gracious dragon Bouriaz?"

Amaease did not give Septabliss a chance to reply.

"Prince Sarabaress," he said, "we are deeply touched by your offer. But I am afraid this is not possible today. There are only certain days during the year on which the holy dragon allows visitors."

"Which days would those be, Septabliss?" asked Prince Sarabaress. A confused and embarrassed Septabliss looked at Amaease.

"It is not fixed," said Amaease. "Allusin informs us of his wishes. Sometimes we must wait many months. Our place as mortals is not to question the nature of the divine choosing. Would you grace our table today, Prince Sarabaress? We hope our simple food will be to your liking."

Prince Sarabaress stood up and said:

"I do recognize the intricacy of the divine plan. Then my offerings shall be left with you, Amaease. I thank you for your graciousness. I remember that the people of Kolallan were famous for their hospitality, and am glad to see that still it is the same. But I am afraid I must start on the road immediately to be back before nightfall."

With those words he bid farewell and left the fortress, escorted by the cavalry.

Septabliss's feelings were hurt, but he considered the meeting a success and the problem resolved.

"Sarabaress is an intelligent and honorable man," said Septabliss. "He accepted our refusal. Surely he can convince Prince Vallusin."

Amaease disagreed.

"When I heard that Prince Sarabaress was coming here I suspected that nothing other than that proposal would make him take such a trip, but later I dismissed the thought and began to hope that his visit would be for investigating the situation here, since he had not been to Kolallan for many years."

"How did you know that he had not visited this town for so long?" asked Septabliss suspiciously.

"It is not so difficult. All you have to do is to ask."

"Whom did you ask, Amaease?"

"People in the street."

"Amaease! Why do you never give me a straight answer?"

"Answers so obvious should never be asked. If you only think before you speak, you do not have to ask silly questions. When did I undermine you, Septabliss?"

"You kept interrupting me today. Your behavior was very humiliating."

"Prince Sarabaress is a knowledgeable man," said Amaease. "I was afraid that you might let him look through the Kot. He would have immediately recognized the false nature of the golden dragon."

"You told the architect and the artist who built that chamber that the golden dragon was the exact replica of our holy dragon. And because the dragon did not wish to be disturbed, he had ordered a replica to be built for him. Why could we not say the same thing to Prince Sarabaress?"

"Because Prince Sarabaress was not under the pledge of secrecy," said Amease. "And we were not in a position to demand such a thing from a prince."

"You should have told me this earlier, so I would have been prepared for it, as I was prepared before encountering the high priest."

"Yes. But I had never encountered a prince like him before, myself. Usually they are arrogant and prudish. He was different."

"What do you think he is going to do?"

"It depends on how persistent the prince is in his decision. We need to find this out."

"How do we find out?"

"Am I being interrogated?" Amaease asked. Disgusted, he left an angry Septabliss behind.

"This is not the first time he has done this," Septabliss thought to himself. "His behavior is offensive and intolerable. He ceaselessly tries to show his superiority. I must show him who is in charge here. In the beginning I thought he was sent from heaven to protect me. Now I suspect that he is here to destroy me. I was in control of everything before he entered my life. Now I am hesitant to say a word without wondering whether or not he would approve. He has stolen my self-confidence. He puts ideas into my head. The fortress looks like a garrison. Now I have to worry that Vanlu might rise up against me. He has made me worry about Allusin, too. So much work! Too many headaches! All we had to do was to hide the worm from the public eye. Maybe Allusin could have married the prince and still fed the worm. I am sure she would have done this for me. She never refuses me. But now this dragon has become a huge problem. Amaease is ruining my life. I should find a way to get rid of him. I need to surround myself with reliable men. My only loyal men so far are these two who bring maidens to me. Amaease is a disgusting person. No one will remain loyal to him."

Those two men were regularly bribed by Amaease to spread the word around town about Septabliss's secret nightly activities. When finally the rumors reached Visseh, after a few abrasive arguments, heartbroken and publicly humiliated, she left her husband. Losing his wife hurt Septabliss's pride, but on the other hand, set him free to openly keep maidens in his house.

The moment Sarabaress reached home he sent for Prince Vallusin.

"My scouts reported," said Sarabaress, "that Allusin was confined in the golden tower, where the dragon lives, and was not allowed visitors. Her personal maid, Pearl, is allowed to attend to her only when her father is present. She is seen picking up the food for herself and for the dragon in front of the entrance to her quarters. She looked healthy but thinner."

"Why is she not allowed any visitors?" asked Prince Vallusin.

"There are quite a few questions for which I do not yet have answers," said Sarabaress as he paced the room slowly, head down and his hands clutched behind him. "I am sure that in due time we will find out. I assure you that deception does not last long. I found Septabliss ignorant and vain. He is just a toy in Amaease's hands.

After Vestur died Amaease became the high priest. He is clever and cunning and is the one who runs the town. They will never consent to this marriage as long as they live. They said that she had devoted her life to the dragon of her own volition."

"This is a lie! I refuse to believe it! I will never accept their rejection!" said the prince.

Sarabaress nodded and continued:

"Together they have robbed the town of its innocence. When we left the fortress I heard a noise and when I asked what it was, they said that it was the dragon's roar. Dragons never roar in that manner. That was the reason why Amaease refused to let me peep through the Kot."

"I will not accept their refusal, uncle. We must free Allusin now!" said the prince impatiently.

"I heard you, my son, and I agree. But I also advise you to know your enemy before you attack."

"What we know is not enough?" asked Prince Vallusin.

"Philosophically it is. We know that they are greedy and greed is the root of all dark forces, because it brings about the passion for consumption and possession. Like a contagious disease it spreads rapidly. But we must be careful. Most of the people of Kolallan are behind them. They have a big army, and the fortress has a hard foundation. It is a stronghold that will be difficult to conquer. We do not know all the details as of yet."

"You draw a grim picture, uncle. But I believe there is no stronghold that cannot be invaded by will and time. I fear for Allusin's life."

"I also have that fear. Yet, Allusin seems not to be in any immediate danger. My advice is to wait, get enough inside information, and then proceed with caution."

"Now that Septabliss and Amaease are aware of my intention to marry Allusin, the longer we wait the harder it may become to rescue her. I suggest that we strike without delay."

"But your men have just come back from a long war," Prince Sarabaress reasoned. "They have been away from their families for too long. They must be weary of war."

"Precisely for this reason we must attack soon. This is exactly what Amaease is counting on. He assumes that with tired and reluctant soldiers we will not start a battle. Surprise is the most effective factor in war. I am a soldier myself. I fight whenever I am ordered. And I am certain that my men are devoted soldiers, too, and will follow me without hesitation."

Prince Sarabaress insisted, "We need to evaluate their army and the strength of its capabilities before we strike. Acting without careful planning could put the entire region in jeopardy."

"I do agree that patience is good, uncle, but I do not agree that postponing this attack will benefit us at all. You taught me yourself that wickedness must be dealt with before it spreads. And now you say that we must delay. How organized can an army be within a year or so? How effectively can troops attack without a good strategy? I believe you are overestimating their power."

"Riches in wicked hands can do wonders. His hired army does not fight for honor or glory but for money to survive. This incentive is great. I am sure they have surrounded themselves with such a force."

"I have met almost all the best commanders from different regions in the battles, and I am certain that none is working for Septabliss," said Prince Vallusin. "We still have time to gather some detailed information on the structure of the fortress and the numbers of his troops and to consult our officers about a plan to invade."

Prince Sarabaress understood that he could not change Prince Vallusin's mind.

As preparation for the battle began, one of Amaease's spies who had infiltrated Prince Sarabaress's guards secretly sent the news of the upcoming battle to him.

The possibility of a fight between his enemies delighted Amaease. He was not certain about the outcome of the battle, but he calculated that at any time he could alter his plans and change sides to join the winner at the end. Destroying the prince was more important than eradicating Septabliss, because Septabliss was already losing face among the army and the townspeople, but to fight a popular young prince was not an easy task. Amaease took the news to Septabliss.

Septabliss was thrilled to see Amaease coming to him with such news and was pleased that he had an army to fight against Prince Vallusin. But Amaease's elaborate system of information-gathering frightened him. Imagining that Amaease might have many informants working for him inside the fortress had a chilling effect on Septabliss.

Septabliss, with Amaease at his side, consulted with his commanding officers on how to use an effective line of attack. They all agreed that under such circumstances the best strategy was to position the army for an ambush. Vantu suggested that he should stay back in case the fortress came under attack. But, Septabliss insisted that Vantu, as a chief officer, must participate in the battle to keep the soldiers' spirits high. Septabliss was counting on his son's carelessness, expecting him to be killed or disabled in the battle, thus removing him as a potential challenger. Septabliss had always had plans to destroy his opponents, including his own son, but had never dared to make it happen. This time he was planning ahead. Amaease was quite happy to back him up.

10

eptabliss's men positioned themselves behind hills all about the rugged terrain far from Kolallan and waited eagerly to combat Prince Vallusin's troops. The rest of the army remained on alert inside the fortress.

To Prince Vallusin's great surprise his army was ambushed. The strings of the bows whistled, shooting a torrential rain of poisonous arrows down, killing hundreds of his men. The cavalry charged and broke apart the lines, making the ranks of his army melt away. It was a wild attack. With a couple of sharp blows Prince Vallusin lost control of the battlefield, and his army was badly crushed. Barzin, who was fighting alongside the prince, was killed shortly before the severely injured prince disappeared from the scene. The battle had begun at sunrise and it ended at sunset.

Though Prince Vallusin's body was not to be found anywhere, many claimed to have seen him slain. Septabliss's army advanced to the castles of both Prince Sarabaress and Prince Vallusin. After one day of fierce resistance and many casualties, the royal castles fell into the hands of their enemies, and Prince Sarabaress was imprisoned in the tower of his own castle.

Septabliss was intoxicated with power. To see Prince Vallusin's army destroyed was beyond his wildest dreams. With such heavenly blessings on his side, he believed he was destined to be a divine ruler. He hoped that Amaease would be satisfied to remain in Prince Sarabaress's castle and mind his own business. He was disappointed though, that his son, Vantu, returned.

Amaease had never lived in a castle. He walked through the halls and the bedrooms, examining every piece of furniture. He stamped on the floors, tapped on the walls, and checked the bookshelves to find out whether or not there were any secret doors or underground passages hidden behind them. He spent the first night in the bedroom of Prince Sarabaress, where he felt very uncomfortable. The room was large and had no access to the outside other than a door opening to a long corridor. There were four windows through which he could see the guards on one side of the towers across the courtyard, and on the other side a vast beautiful garden. After locking the door and closing the curtains, he removed a blanket from the large bed. He pulled it over his head, covered his body, and curled up on the floor near the fireplace.

Riding through the battle, watching the bloody and dismembered bodies of his enemies had filled the hungry stomachs of his childhood giants and monsters. He felt satisfied and did not have the urge to get up and nibble that night. He thought about Prince Sarabaress, wondering how he felt that night. His gentle demeanor reminded him of his own father. But unlike his father's degrading attitude, Prince Sarabaress had distinguished manners, which appealed to Amaease.

"He must be miserable," he thought. "He has lost everything. I should pay him a visit tomorrow. It will be interesting to hear what he has to say. He is too proud to ask for forgiveness. Besides, he knows that I will not release him under any circumstances. Just like me, he has no family now. Most of his relatives were killed or have fled. Maybe, like Septabliss, he does not have any feelings for the prince. But he seems like a kind person. This makes him vulnerable and easily manipulated. My sisters manipulated my father all the time. He had no courage to disagree with them or prevent them from beating me. Women are ruthless, unforgiving, and vengeful. He could not protect me. Fools and cowards deserve to die."

When Amaease awoke, the very first order of business was to visit Prince Sarabaress. Upon his arrival, the prince was standing behind a barred window, watching the sky. He did not turn to see who was entering his cell until Amaease spoke.

"Good morning, Prince Sarabaress!"

Prince Sarabaress gently turned around. "Good morning, Amaease," he said. He was grief stricken but his voice was calm and indifferent.

"Last night I was wondering how you must be feeling," said Amaease.

"I slept very well, thank you. And I did not wonder about your feelings."

"Princes and kings never lose sleep over the little people. Do they?

"There are no little people in the eyes of true kings and princes, but there are evil people. And they can be recognized immediately."

"I am glad that imprisonment did not disrupt your sleep. I confess that I did not sleep very well in this damned castle. Its structure reveals the life of vain minds—representative of the privileged class; it does not appeal to me. I must see that it is razed."

"I do not feel that I am in a prison. No one can take away my freedom. Even by taking my life, you would only set my spirit free. You cannot win. But it is a pity that even in a castle you feel like a prisoner."

"So often I have listened to similar preaching. Statements such as this come from the mind of a broken spirit. What a pity indeed! I had more respect for you before. But now I am convinced that your humility comes from failure and defeat rather than success. You have nothing to show for your life. You have not achieved anything. You were born a prince, but you will die the prisoner of a cobbler's son."

"I was born a prince and I will die a free man. You were born a free man, but you will die the prisoner of a worm. Man has always a choice. Peerbabu also was the son of a cobbler, but he is a free spirit now."

A wave of murderous rage swept through Amaease's body. From his bloodshot eyes arrows of hatred shot out at Sarabaress. White foam frothed from his mouth. Transformed, he stood motionless for a few moments; his mind jammed with tortured memories of his childhood. The tyranny and oppression of his past tormentors paraded in front of his eyes. But the thought of Peerbabu being the son of a cobbler amused him, and with that he got control of his emotions. Collecting his thoughts, he smiled at Prince Sarabaress, who was staring at him with curiosity.

"Do you need anything to be brought to you, Prince Sarabaress?" asked Amaease, coldly.

"Only two books which are on my desk, if possible. Thank you, Amaease!" Prince Sarabaress was amazed by the fast-changing expression on Amaease's face. "He is the devil himself, transforming every second!" he thought.

Amaease left the cell and ordered the books to be taken to Prince Sarabaress. He also ordered wine and food to be served to the prince, in the fashion to which the prince was accustomed.

For the rest of the day, he reminded himself, "Anger must never take hold of me. It is a sign of weakness. Men like Sarabaress dangerously consume my energy. I must go back to my own chamber in Kolallan. That is the only safe place for me now. This castle is not properly secured. The rooms are too bright and the walls reject me."

hen Prince Vallusin opened his eyes, he was in a comfortable bed in a room with light coming through a large window high above his head. He was covered with white linen and a white woolen blanket on which his dynastic motif was embroidered. On a wooden shelf, in an elaborately decorated brass incense holder, frankincense burned.

He sat on the bed trying to collect his memory. He had been in a battle and had been hit with arrows in his shoulder and chest. He remembered the pain from a deep ax wound in his left thigh. The man had approached him from behind, striking both him and his horse. He remembered falling down, hitting one attacker with his sword, and the other with? . . . He could remember nothing more, except a vision of some white clouds hanging over him, warmly touching his face. He stood up to examine himself. He was wearing a long white fine linen robe exactly like the ones he used to wear at home. There was no sign of any wounds on his body! He had no pain and felt quite healthy.

"Where am I? How did I end up here? Where is this place? What happened to my army?"

"You are with a friend. The rest is of no importance," a warm but commanding voice replied.

In front of him stood Peerbabu.

"I know who you are," the prince said. "I have seen you a couple of times around Kolallan and Assal. But whenever I tried to approach you, you suddenly disappeared. I have asked my uncle about you. He said that when the time came I would get to know you. Who brought me here? What happened to my army?"

"I am afraid I have no good news for you. The spies had warned your enemies of your attack and they planned to ambush you. Your army was totally defeated. Their devotion and bravery did not withstand the surprise assault of Septabliss's well-equipped soldiers. They captured both castles, and Prince Sarabaress is being held prisoner in his own tower. It was actually Barzin who, by giving up his own life, spared me a few more minutes to save you. Prince Sarabaress and I knew that someday he was going to sacrifice his life for you."

"If you knew he was going to be killed, then why did you not stop him from taking part in the battle?" asked the prince.

"Certain courses of events cannot be changed. His fate was sealed with you from the very beginning. He was the sun going down so that you could rise the next day. It was exactly at sunset when he attempted your rescue, but was shot by a poisonous arrow. In fact, if you were not wearing this necklace and this pendant, I could not have saved you either."

"My uncle gave it to me before I went to war. Prior to the battle he asked me if I was still wearing it. I know the beads are of amber, but I know not of what the pendant is made."

"From the time Prince Sarabaress held you in his arms he made it his business to protect you at all cost. The pendant is made of Padzahr stone, rare and difficult to obtain."

"Is it a natural stone?" asked the prince.

"No, it is not. If a ten-year-old stag eats many snakes, a great heat engulfs his body. To cool it off, he rushes to the water to soak himself up to his eyes for a few hours. When he leaves the water, if he is immediately captured and killed, this stone can be removed from his stomach. It protects a person from poisoning."

"Did you advise him to give this to me?"

"No. Prince Sarabaress is well-schooled in minerals and has mastered the medicinal techniques of herbs."

"Then why did you never take him as an apprentice? You seem to have a high opinion of him."

"Every individual has a particular mission in life. His job was to bring you up. It was a big responsibility."

"Why did you save me? How long have I been here?"

Peerbabu looked at him affectionately. "You ask too many questions. You have been very ill. There were days that I thought you would not make it. But your vital signs were good. You have been here almost twenty days."

"My uncle tried to warn me," said Prince Vallusin sadly. "I never listened! There was this uncontrollable urge in me to rescue Allusin. I felt very heroic."

"A romantic hero fights for himself, but a true hero's goal is to defeat the dark forces both inside himself and in the outside world. There was a strong fear of losing Allusin in you, was there not?"

"Yes! It was fear of losing her. Losing my very soul. You are right!" said the prince, surprised. "But look at me now! I am a man without glory, without an army, and without a loving family. My best friend, Barzin, is dead. This weight will be on my shoulders for the rest of my life. And Allusin, whom I wanted to rescue, is still in prison. Furthermore, the dark force is stronger than ever before."

"Should the evil deeds of earthly men be a hundred times worse, they would not rise up so high as the good deeds of heaven, so the ancient scriptures say," said Peerbabu with authority. "You came back from war a hero. This image appealed to you and you took yourself too seriously. But a true hero fights for the truth, sacrificing even his own life for the good of others. People are not tools to be used or sacrificed for selfish reasons. There is no glory in war, and neither side wins, because lives are lost in battle, homes ruined, and pastures destroyed under the feet of horses and the wheels of chariots. But to put your mind at ease, I have seen Allusin twice. She knows that you are alive and well. She is unhappy, yet enduring. Her isolation must not be prolonged. I shall pay her a visit soon."

"Thank you, Peerbabu, for bringing such joy to my heart! But how did you enter the fortress? May I go along with you this time?"

"No, you may not. And stop asking so many questions! The worm has an uncanny sense of smell. It can locate human beings at a great distance even while it is asleep. It only opens its mouths when Allusin feeds it. When slightly suspicious it can attack anyone, even Allusin. It has done so on my two visits there. Only Saiparak can handle it with his ferocious barking. But if the worm were to be threatened and become angry, even Saiparak might be defeated by its unleashed rage. I have given Allusin a potion to put in its food to reduce its sense of smell. Both the dosage and the frequency of administration had to be very gradual so it would not detect the potion. The worm's fury frightened her the first time I was there, but she was much calmer on my second visit."

"Without an army how are we to conquer the fortress?"

"First with patience, my prince. Battles are not won only by the riders on swift horses with their nostrils quivering, or the flight of a thousand sharp arrows crowding the sky, or the force of a thousand men with steel hammers pounding. These are only some aspects of war. Soldiers need incentive to act bravely and the enthusiasm to take up the challenge. Officers need to believe in the cause and love their commanders in order to convince soldiers that losing their lives would be for a just end. But above all, the leaders should act not in their own interest, but for the good of the people. The right time, the right place, and intelligence are vital for the outcome of war as well. Young men are fast in actions, quick in reaction, and often rash in judgment. Though this is the nature of youth, it can be improved upon with deeper inner experience," Peerbabu said calmly.

"Quick thinking and fast decisions have brought me success, but they seem to be the source of my downfall as well."

"That which causes your rise causes your fall," said Peerbabu. "Now I am certain that you are destined to serve our people and this land. I will lead you on the path of initiation to become a selfless ruler who is compassionate, just, and forgiving."

"I swear upon my honor that I will be patient and follow your instructions without further questions."

"Well then, it is settled," said Peerbabu with a fatherly smile.

12

or days Peerbabu took the prince to the woods, hills, and mountains. As they walked the master showed his apprentice the uses of different herbs to make potions to cure various ailments.

"Veneration for nature is the first step to take. Yielding to the natural spirits is the second step. When one reaches inner balance the human soul connects to the souls of plants and animals. Beasts, by the look in one's eyes, and plants, by the touch of one's hands, understand whether one is a friend or a foe. Their compassionate nature will guide the person through the woods, and little by little minerals, plants, and animals reveal their secrets. One must coordinate his rhythm of life with the rhythm of his surroundings to take the third step."

"When the rhythm becomes harmonious why do you still have to put it into words? I heard you asking permission from some flowers prior to cutting them," said the prince.

"Each word has its special resonance. Each tone has its particular effect. We humans communicate through sound, and the tone of voice helps us evaluate another person's affections. The creatures of the forests, water, air, and fire will serve you when you learn how to communicate with them. You walk on the soil, which is theirs. You use products of their labor freely. Do you not think it only fair, if not necessary, to make an effort to verbally ask their permission when you want to use them for your own benefit?"

"I do understand your point, but if we do not kill animals and do not use plants, how can humans survive?" asked the prince.

"Nature provides man for his need but not for his greed. Animals also kill to survive. Plants assault too and can be aggressive defending themselves."

"But we need to make arrows to use in wars. Do you call that excessive usage? Our horses and carriages pass through plains and prairies. Is it possible to ask permission and forgiveness from all plants smashed along the way?"

"Wars are based on greed. Wars destroy not only the harmony in nature but plant the seed of revenge and hatred in human hearts that grows with each generation. Vengeance causes the soul to fall and therefore prevents the spirit from rising to its destined abode. But at the same time, we know that even in the animal kingdom, territories must be defended, as the survival of the species depends on it. To recognize the legitimacy of war one needs deep understanding. The higher authorities know that when deception and injustice are not dealt with in societies, anger and revenge are the outcome. This creates a vicious cycle of destruction. Resisting injustice prevents the advancement of the dark force. The moment it stops growing, it begins to deteriorate."

"How can we communicate with them to make it clear what we do is for good and not for evil?"

"Mother Earth cannot be fooled. One cannot control the eruption of volcanoes or prevent tornados, floods, or famine. Man must not make Mother Earth angry! Many seekers have lost their lives by overconfidence and by selfish interpretations of the rules of nature. Many have tried to exhibit their superiority over it. They all have failed. Forces of nature act with broad consciousness. One must use them with great caution. Animals and plants retain their memories through generations and transformations, which to us seem like thousands of years. But time itself is an illusion. When injured by one's hand they neither forget nor forgive. When ignored and offended, instinctively they assault. This is only one small part of their secret for survival. One has to approach them with respect, honoring their existence as one honors one's own. This plant has a healing effect on bruised and broken bones. If taken internally for a long period of time, it can lead to serious disease. I have used its poultices on your wounds.

"Human nature has experienced the world of vegetation, but it has not yet experienced ours. So it is up to us to take the first step and begin the dialogue. Plants exhibit their joy and sadness, their hunger and their thirst, as we do. When our own plant and animal nature is revealed to us we understand their language, receive their messages, and benefit from their guidance. Look at this plant! For its protection it is covered with stinging hairs, which cause irritation and inflammation of the skin. But its friendly nature also offers the cure in its flowers. Like human beings they also have two sides!

"Consciousness travels through darkness to reach light. Opposites create life and make the world go on. The dark force, which disguises itself in all four worlds of the mineral, vegetation, animal, and human, is hard to identify by the inexperienced and untrained soul. Beautiful stones and flowers can poison the body instantaneously if one is not familiar with their nature. Miniature and harmless-looking animals can kill without mercy. Look at this plant! I used its blossoms and the yellow juice from its stem to calm the pain in your body when you were gravely ill. One can use its roots, leaves, stem, and the flowers as tonic, but the leaves need to be gathered when young.

"The mountains will teach you how to explore your own nature until it becomes the source of your never-failing strength, the spring of your ever-increasing wisdom. This plant, for instance, blossoms on the first day of each month. So when you lose track of time, it can be a good reminder."

Peerbabu taught the prince how to coordinate his senses with the rhythm of his surroundings to keep himself from danger. He made him sit in the woods with his eyes closed during the day and stay awake during the night to listen to the sounds of the woods. Prince Vallusin learned to differentiate between various species of birds, communicate with the beasts, sense the crawling reptiles, and smell flowers from far distances.

At night, Peerbabu took Prince Vallusin to the roof of his tower to sit for hours and concentrate on his breathing in order to be able to control it. He taught him how to follow the wind, how to chase clouds, how to know when the rain will fall and when the storm will hit. He taught him how to track the stars, and how to use the power of the planets when they are aligned, and when and how to praise them to please their nature.

"Although in creation mankind is superior to the stars, the stars rule over us and may hurt us if we let them. The golden key to the secret of our past is held in those planets. You see, you and I have the luxury of making mistakes and learning from them, but they are not given this chance. They must perform ceaselessly, passionately, and precisely with no errors. Imagine the calamities that would befall the Earth if one morning our sun decided to rise one second late! If Saturn chose to move faster! Or if the moon became playful and remained full for nights on end! When you begin to respect their dedication and their endurance, then you will discover the forces in yourself and thus become your own master. No one will be able to rule over you ever again."

One night Peerbabu pointed to the center of the roof and said to the prince, "I want you to sit right here and meditate!"

The prince sat there in silence with his eyes half opened. He began to control his breathing in the manner he was taught. Gradually he felt weightless, as if floating in the air. He heard Peerbabu's voice chanting a hymn:

O Divine Spirit!
You are the source of creation!
You are the cause of creation!
Yours is the victory in creations both good and evil!
All men pray to you:
Men of faith.
Men of war.
Men of pastures.
O endless space!
Your kingdom ever increasing!
O endless time!
Your wisdom ever increasing!
O endless force!
Your strength ever increasing!
You are swift, the swiftest!
You are the gentlest!
You are hard, the hardest!
You are the softest!
You are strong, the strongest!
You are without sufferings!
You are brave, the bravest!
You are without corruption and everlasting!
You are without partners and everlasting!
You are in all, and all is in you.

Prince Vallusin saw his parents and his little sister moving freely through blossoming fruit trees shimmering in the sunlight. It was exhilarating to see their cheerful faces. He followed them and felt deeply content to be so close to them. Gradually, the world disappeared from his sight. His skin felt the darkness of the night. He heard the voice of silence and the movement of the stars. He tasted sweetness in the cup of the moon. He smelled the sunrise. And then he opened his eyes wide. The sun was rising on the horizon.

He went downstairs. Peerbabu put bread, honey, and milk on the table and left the room. Prince Vallusin had such a great appetite; it was as if he had not eaten for days. He did not feel like talking and was glad that Peerbabu had left.

In the evening when he mentioned it, Peerbabu said:

"Words are useless for those who converse with their hearts, listen with their eyes, and hear with their minds."

The next night Peerbabu asked the prince to follow him to a cave.

The entrance to the cave was behind an old oak tree, under which people left their sick relatives. It was quite hidden from ordinary eyes. It was so low that they had to crawl in order to pass through it, but just inside the cave there was a long, tall, wide corridor. Once they were in the corridor, Peerbabu lit a torch that he had been carrying. The corridor led to an enormous terrace, at the end of which was a boat floating upon a lake. As Peerbabu and the prince stepped into the boat, Peerbabu gave the torch to Prince Vallusin and began to paddle. He guided the boat through many channels, some enormously wide with the height of a seven-story building, and some narrow and so short that they had to bend in order to cross. The prince was awed by the elaborate and distinct shapes of animals that appeared to be sculpted in stone upon the walls. There were doves, crows, crocodiles, snakes, mountain goats, and even elephants covering the surface of the walls, glittering wildly in the light. Prince Vallusin looked into the water. There were no fish. There was an eerie feeling about this place. He was beginning to feel uncomfortable, when he heard Peerbabu's voice.

"Fear is an illusion. Like a shadow it does not exist. Evil lives on fear, on greed, on doubt, on hatred, on anger, on jealousy, and on lust. When it is not fed, it begins to lose energy."

"It is hard to see it coming. Many a time it just appears out of nowhere," the prince observed.

"The bad seeds are naturally in the soil like the good. With some watering they all sprout. If the climate and the surroundings are suitable for that particular seed, it blossoms. Mortals cannot uproot evil, but they can stop its growth by not feeding it."

"How do you stop feeding it?"

"By resisting it and by trusting its opposite force: Desire to do goodness. Desire to be righteous. Desire to be content. Desire to be grateful. Desire to be truthful. Desire to be giving and desire to forgive. These desires bring courage to the heart and combat wickedness. The very thought of not surrendering to evil reduces its energy. Desiring a little less and giving a little more are all one needs to begin the journey. To take the second step is as important as the first, but there is no last step. An evil mind is always suspicious and doubtful, because it projects its own nature upon the others. So trust is the first step to take, and you have taken it," said Peerbabu.

His voice echoed through the empty halls, vibrating back to Prince Vallusin. Peerbabu stopped at the foot of a tall staircase and said, "From here on you are on your own. Climb these stairs and you will find your way out if your heart so wishes. I know my way back. You should find yours."

With that he slowly paddled away.

Prince Vallusin climbed up the 360 steps and found himself on a rotund veranda, surrounded by steep cliffs. He looked around. There was a huge symbol of a male organ, as if carved in stone, which rose to the ceiling in the middle of the cliff on the east side. As he moved to look around, the torch went out and he was left in total darkness. Questions crowded his mind.

"Why did he leave me here alone? Why did the torch go out so rapidly? How can I find my way back? Why has it suddenly become so cold? How can I climb down those slippery steps? If I do make my way down, how am I going cross those channels? Why did he take the boat? Why did he not wait for me?"

"Evil feeds on fear!" He heard the echoes of Peerbabu's voice. "The world of darkness is crowded with doubts and is busy with internal dialogues. Through a clear conscience, a quiet mind commands actions and does not react."

"I failed Uncle Sarabaress. I will not fail Peerbabu. My mind is betraying me again."

He sat down, closed his eyes, and began to control his rapid breathing. He felt the dampness of the place seep into his bones. It was a cloudy day. The ground was covered with ice and the wind was howling. A chill went through his spine. He saw the attack on his father's camp. He saw the spear going through his body in front of the tent. He saw his mother's head cut off. He saw his little sister dragged behind a horse. Carnage spread all around burning tents. He yelled in rage and stood up.

"Such monstrosity should not be left unpunished. I will see that it never happens again!"

Peerbabu's words echoed:

"Evil rises in anger!"

"I should not be provoked by anger. I should not be lured into harsh reaction. I should not yield to this kind of deception! But how can I leave this place without any light?" he shouted with all his strength.

"If owls can see in the dark, so can we." The prince recalled Peerbabu's words.

He sat down again and began to breathe calmly, listening to the silence.

This time he saw his father's army invading the tribe. He saw screaming women and children being captured and taken away for slavery in front of their angry and helpless husbands and fathers, who shouted, "Have pity on us! There was drought! There was famine! We could not pay taxes!"

"Such horrendous injustice! This must never happen in a kingdom!"

He was deeply disturbed by the guilt invading his heart. Peerbabu's words rang in his ears:

"Recognizing the injustice sheds light on the mind, but only by the right actions will justice be done, not by maintaining a sense of guilt."

Again Prince Vallusin tried to calm his agitated mind by eradicating all negative feelings. When he brought it to a standstill, there was a void!

A sudden warm breeze engulfed his body. The chill was gone. He opened his eyes and looked up. He saw the seven stars of the Big Dipper right above his head circling around the North Star, forming a broken cross in seven colors like a spinning wheel, creating space within which galaxies were born and the four seasons began. He saw waters surrounded by a circle of fire and in the midst of the water he saw a throne. He heard the music of the spheres. His heart was filled with joy. He stood up and looked around. It was not as dark as he had imagined previously. He could see a couple of narrow steps down and a pathway leading out. He followed the path. There were two rooms on each side. He continued and finally entered a circular room with an altar. Motifs of the sun and the moon were engraved on its wall. There stood Peerbabu solemnly. He nodded gently and made a gesture to be followed. He passed through a couple of narrow and intricate corridors and out of the cave.

"I was beginning to wonder," said Peerbabu gently.

"Why? It did not take me long, did it?" asked the prince, surprised.

"Almost a week. My estimate was five days." Peerbabu said.

"It did not seem that long. But—"

Peerbabu did not let the prince finish his sentence.

"In time, my prince. We have work to do and places to go, and we need to make some preparations."

"I only need to ask you one question and no more," said the prince.

"You have an inquisitive nature, my prince. This will be the last one for a long time to come. What is it?"

"What made you choose me?"

"I knew that question was coming. You sensed it when I said that I was wondering. You see, my prince, esoteric knowledge should be stored away and kept hidden until the right candidate is found. You had the right birthmark, but deceit works in many crooked ways disguised as truth. Even masters have fallen from grace. With one mistake, one can lose all. You have taken the first step and have passed the test, but the hardship has only begun."

"I am ready for any trial, any hardship, whatever you have planned for me."

"I am glad to hear that, but your young body also needs to be nourished and rewarded in order not to interfere with the growth of your soul. No matter how high and for how long birds fly in the sky, they must come down to earth for feeding."

"You sound mysterious, Peerbabu!"

"You have not asked me how we are going to rescue Allusin."

"I thought when the time came, you would let me know. I am certain that you will not let her perish in that tower."

"Then, I bow to the achievement of a noble and trusting soul, who is no longer enslaved by his emotions, and whose argumentative mind is under his control," said Peerbabu. "We cannot conquer the fortress in conventional ways; we must have careful planning and preparation. On the other hand, it is important that we rescue Allusin fast. It is time for you to know how the invisible dark force operates. Septabliss depends on the worm to maintain his vitality, and the worm grows by sucking Allusin's life energy. If Allusin dies, the worm and Septabliss die, too. To deal with Amaease is another matter that we will discuss later, but unfortunately, there is not much time left for Allusin."

"How much time do we have?" asked the prince.

"Yet enough, I should say. But we need to accelerate the pace of our plan. Soon I will pay a visit to Amaease. Things will move much faster if he agrees to cooperate. Septabliss is a fly fallen into Amaease's web. Amaease has led Septabliss to a sordid way of life. Because of that he has lost respect among his commanders, soldiers, and even people in the streets. Amaease and Septabliss both assume that you are dead, so they do not expect any action to be taken by anyone, except the king. Amaease may have calculated that the king is not willing to spend more of his already depleted treasury on another battle. We must take advantage of their misinformation to execute our plan."

13

ne night as Amaease was sitting in his chamber reading, Peerbabu appeared. Once again Amaease's heart was invaded by fear. Even as a little child when his sisters threw him in the smelly storage pit, he never cried or pleaded to be freed. The moment they closed the heavy lid and left him in total darkness, he began to imagine plots against the ones whom he loathed. In his mind he played the role of a giant who smashed his enemies' heads against mountains, or devoured them alive. Sometimes he became a monster, scaring little children to death as they walked with their mothers. He longed to paralyze his sisters with fright. Enjoying these fantasies, he stayed in the rotten pit for hours, as if he were in a rose garden.

When he saw Peerbabu standing before him, he opened and closed his mouth without a sound. He felt as if his being had disappeared, leaving him with just a shrunken skin. His body froze. His eyes glazed. He was not sure whether Peerbabu was real, a ghost, or a part of his own runaway imagination. His hands fell lifelessly onto his lap. There was no strength left in his feet.

Smiling, Peerbabu approached him and said, "Believe me, I am real! Have you never seen an old man before?"

Amaease did not move. He felt numb all over. His heart was barely beating and his eyes stayed wide open without blinking. Peerbabu came closer. With one hand he closed Amaease's eyes, and with the other he touched Amaease's head until warmth flowed through his body, bringing back the sensation to his limbs. When Peerbabu removed his hands, Amaease opened his eyes, feeling strangely tranquil. He looked at Peerbabu and mumbled:

"You must be Peerbabu!"

Peerbabu nodded.

"Were you hiding in my room before I locked the door?" asked Amaease.

"No," said Peerbabu, calmly.

Amaease stood up. Slowly he walked toward a bookcase. Three times he kicked the bottom row of the books in the middle. The bookcase revolved, revealing a short door behind it. He pushed the door. The door was locked. He reached under his robe and pulled out a leather string with two small keys dangling. He opened the door, bent, and looked down at a spiral staircase. He locked the door and returned to his seat.

"How did you enter this room then?" he asked.

Peerbabu laughed heartily. "When I am anxious to see my friends, walls and locks do not stop me."

"I never had enough time to learn this art," said Amaease.

"It is not something one learns. It is the person one becomes."

"I do not understand."

"I know. I do not expect you to," said Peerbabu.

"Why are you here?" asked Amaease.

"In some aspects of our future plans we share the same goal. I want to destroy the worm. You want to destroy Septabliss before he destroys you."

Amaease did not react to what Peerbabu had said.

Peerbabu gazed into his eyes and continued:

"But you cannot touch Septabliss as long as the worm lives. Because if something happens to Septabliss, Allusin will not feed the worm and the worm will die. People worship the false dragon. Its presence gives them spiritual support and so they bring offerings as long as the dragon keeps roaring. If you do not help me to destroy the worm, I will not help you to take Septabliss's position. He is itching to have you killed and I can make sure that he succeeds."

"Why do you want to kill the dragon? Why do you choose me instead of Septabliss? If the dragon dies, then whose roaring will convince people that he is alive and can perform miracles?"

"I have my personal reasons to destroy the worm. Maybe someday I shall tell you. You have turned Septabliss into a superstitious clown who is easy to manipulate. It is true that nowadays he believes in himself more than he believes in the worm, but still he is deeply connected to it and will not consent to its destruction. That is why I have chosen to make a deal with you.

"I also know that you have begun to have doubts about the worm being the source of power and slowly you will detach yourself from it. Somehow you know that if the worm dies, Septabliss will perish with him. You must have calculated that whoever runs Kolallan will be the future ruler of this country. Because once the aging king dies, his army will not remain loyal to just any chief commander and will divide, unless the right person takes charge of the situation. I can make the fake golden dragon roar in the same manner as the worm. If you step outside with me, I will prove it. I assure you that no one will be able to tell the difference."

"It is not necessary. I know that you can. I accept your offer," said Amaease. "After all, we are both sons of cobblers. Perhaps you and I are secretly connected. You must have your hidden ambitions, too. For the time being your only superiority is this art of suddenly appearing, but I assure you that someday I will be able to perform that as well. Tell me, how do you want me to help you?"

Peerbabu described his plan and left behind a confused Amaease.

Amaease lay on the floor, pulled a blanket over his head, and agitated, began to think.

"What nonsense! He thinks I am stupid. What he does is sheer magic. If I had learned this particular art of sudden appearance and departures, no one in the world could stop me. He was privileged to have come across a good teacher. I wonder how old Peerbabu is. He is vibrant and energetic. There is no sign of old age in him. With that technique he must have seen the real dragon. But he referred to it as the worm and not the dragon. This must be Septabliss's secret! I should have known better!

"Peerbabu was right. In the beginning I did believe that the dragon was the source of power, but now it does not matter any more. Who cares whether it is a worm or a dragon, so long it continues to bring income to me? It will be a long time before it disappoints these imbeciles. The treasury is loaded with enough gold to support a large army and take over the country. After that, I do not care what they believe in. Still I cannot figure out the connection between the ring, the dog, the worm, and Allusin. He is up to something! I must find a way to solve this puzzle. My informants have no access to Peerbabu and are inadequate in gathering information about him. I am certain though that he is merely a magician, whose scary look forces him to hide from public view. He admitted that he could not stop me once Septabliss and Allusin are out of my way. He is aware of the fact that he is useless in battles; that is the reason he tries to snatch Allusin out of the fortress by tricks. He is a fool not to know that by annihilating Septabliss and the worm and by removing Allusin from my path, he is digging his own grave. Soon I will make him disappear for good."

14

Prince Vallusin rode to the neighboring town of Sanrod to meet with Nerssey, who had been under his command during the war and had a small army. Nerssey was astounded when he saw the prince.

"What a delightful surprise, my prince! I heard you were killed in the battle with Septabliss's army. Everything happened so fast that by the time we learned about it, it was too late for any action. The two castles had already fallen into enemy hands."

"It was a misjudgment on my part," said the prince. "My hasty decision brought about a disastrous conclusion. Later on I plan to go and seek help from the king, but for now I do not want word to get out that I am alive. I require fifty-two of your most trusted men to accompany me on a short trip. You will be informed in case our plan fails so that you can send your dispatcher to take the news to the king," said Prince Vallusin.

When the prince returned with fifty-two soldiers, he was amazed by the enormous job Peerbabu had done in his absence. Around the hills, Peerbabu had organized a large caravan to ride with him to visit Septabliss in Kolallan.

The prince disguised himself as a middle-aged trader and arrived with his large entourage. They were all clothed in gold-embroidered silk and sat upon saddles inlaid with precious stones. Loads of merchandise followed them in wagons and carts drawn by camels and horses.

Impressed, Septabliss ordered the fortress to be opened, and he placed them in the guest quarters. That night he invited them all to a banquet in order to show off his wealth and power.

"I have been on the road all my life," said the prince, "and I have never seen such a magnificent fortress before. I daresay only Chinese emperors may afford luxurious living equal to this."

"My dear friend, the Chinese have ruled for thousands of years," boasted Septabliss. "It took me only a couple to come up with this marvel. With the blessings of our holy dragon, I may well be a heavenly emperor soon."

"Blessings indeed! Heaven knows to whom blessings should be endowed. You must be a favorite of the Gods," said the prince.

"How insightful you are, my friend! There are not many men intelligent enough to recognize a divine presence when they come across one. Divinities must live among men, listen to their complaints, heal their wounds, and overcome the drought, such as I have done. This is the obvious reality." Septabliss moved his hands in the air, tasting each word that came out of his mouth with ecstasy.

"You seem to have a divine mission to fulfill. I am a man of pleasure and will pray to anyone who provides me with it. I can pray to blessed ones like you," said the prince, pretending to be affected by too much wine. "I believe Gods created men for their own pleasure, and they are generous to those who recognize it. Look at yourself! Look at me! And look at all those wretched people who go to temple every day to pray."

Septabliss found the prince to his liking.

"I wish my son were like you. He does not know how to make money. I have to provide him with everything. But men like you make a difference in societies. It gives me such pleasure to entertain you and your friends. You can stay with us as long as you wish. The fortress is at your disposal. To show you my satisfaction, tomorrow I will give you a chance to pay tribute to our holy dragon Bouriaz. It is a rare privilege, you know, but as my special guest you are welcome to it. You will be provided with whatever you and your companions need. But unfortunately I need to go home now. I must spend the nights there. I have certain divine duties to perform."

"I have enjoyed your company. I wish you could stay longer. I am not in a habit of retiring early, but tonight I may do so as I promised my friends a fabulous hunting day tomorrow. Will you come along?" asked the prince.

"I may join you later on. If not, then you are invited to come to my house tomorrow night to enjoy some great entertainment. You will be pleased with what I have to offer. I know the delicate taste of lofty people like you."

"I am told that the beauty of Kolallan's maidens is beyond compare."

"You will not be disappointed! By the way, you may roam around the lake and the garden. For security reasons no one is allowed to do that, but I will order my guards not to disturb you as long as you are here. The lake is more attractive when the moon is out, but when it is pitch dark, like tonight, there is a mysterious feeling about it. You should experience it."

Since Amaease was not present to undermine his decisions or humiliate him, Septabliss went overboard to display his authority. Overwhelmed by feelings of self-importance, he abandoned his suspicious nature completely.

When Septabliss left, the prince's men scattered across the garden, pretending to be drunk. Gradually, as if they were lost, they entered the towers, carrying jugs of wine mixed with sleeping potion. In case some refused to drink wine, Peerbabu had also put sleeping potion in the food, which was prepared for the guards of the seven towers. The prince's fifty-two men wore the armor and the helmets of the fifty-two guards over their clothes. In order not to attract the attention of the other guards, who were on the lookout on the walls surrounding the fortress, they stood guard themselves until dawn.

Two nights before the event, Peerbabu had paid a visit to Allusin, preparing her for what she had to do and telling her what to expect. So, Allusin was impatiently standing by her bedroom window, waiting. When she saw the prince below, she lowered one of the ropes, which Peerbabu had already tied around her bed, for the prince to climb up. They embraced for a long time without uttering a word. Tears of joy drowned her face. For fear of awakening the worm, she whispered:

"Many a time I pleaded with heaven to turn me into a wild goose so with your arrow I could fall at your feet. Time and time again I begged to become a river so I might embrace you when you bathed. My heart, though sad, never lost hope, even at the shortest cruelest day or the longest torturous night of the year."

"My sweet Allusin!" the prince whispered back. "You are the divine gift to me. Remembering your smile persuaded me to overcome death. Your shining eyes guided me beyond the twilight of doubts during my initiation trial."

They spent a sleepless night waiting for Peerbabu to come. There was a happy smile on Peerbabu's face when he saw them together.

"Everything is well arranged," he said. "This is how we are going to execute the plan. You, Prince Vallusin, and I will go to the worm's room and stand behind it. Allusin will bring the food a little bit earlier than usual, while it is asleep. The smell of the food will awaken him and he will open his three mouths simultaneously. Immediately, we shall pour the hot solder into his mouths and leave the gallery. When you reach the ground, horses will be there to take you out of the fortress. You have only a few minutes to leave the tower before the worm will explode and the guards will wake up. Allusin should wear this garment to disguise herself as a man. All must leave the fortress at the same time. I do not wish any unnecessary bloodshed."

"How will you get out of the fortress, Peerbabu?" asked Allusin.

Peerbabu smiled, "The way I came in!"

"How about Saiparak?" asked Allusin again.

"Do not worry, my girl! Saiparak knows his way out of this tower quite well. He will join us later."

15

maease stayed away from the fortress all day as he had agreed with Peerbabu. He was informed about the arrival of the caravan in town and was eager to find out the rest of Peerbabu's plot.

Early before sunrise, as the plan was, Amaease went to the white tower and said to the maidens serving food to the dragon, "It is the holy dragon's wish that today a special warm food be served. Fire should be lit on the golden tower close to the entrance, so by the time it reaches his holy mouth, the food does not get cold. Today I have prepared the food myself. From tomorrow on, in case he desires to continue to have the same meal, I will teach you how to cook it yourselves. It is complicated: the right temperature and the proper ingredients are of utmost importance. I have no doubt that with your devotion to him you will learn it within one week. I shall be here every day to teach and supervise you until I am certain that you have fully learned the technique. We do not want to displease the divine dragon."

Three large braziers were brought in, and on them were placed three large pots. Amaease filled the pots with solder concealed under honey and poppy seeds and brought them to boil so that Allusin could rush them to the worm.

The worm was restless all night. It become more agitated as it feebly sensed the presence of others in the gallery.

As Allusin was picking up the food to carry it inside, Amaease said in a loud voice, "May your journey be blessed!"

Allusin carried the three heavy pots inside the worm's chamber and placed them each before its mouths. She was exhausted. As she approached the worm and tried to hold the pot up to pour the hot solder into the opened mouth of the worm, she collapsed under the heavy weight of the pot, which fell to the ground. The worm raised its head and began to move violently. Peerbabu and the prince quickly poured the contents of the other two pots into the worm's mouth. Then the prince rushed to lift Allusin before the worm could harm her. Peerbabu held the worm's head in place by pressing down his dragonhead cane until the prince carried Allusin out of the chamber. Before leaving the scene he said, "It is your fight now, Saiparak. Go for the middle head!"

As the prince held Allusin, Peerbabu tied the ropes around them and gently let them down until they reached the ground. There was no time for Allusin to change her clothes, so the prince wrapped his cloak around her and covered her head.

The worm had raised its heads and was screeching. The barking Saiparak jumped on the worm and went for the jugular of its middle head, which was still moving. Each time Saiparak bit deeper into its neck, the worm flung him against the wall. The fight went on until the worm's body exploded. The bleeding body of Saiparak also lay dead in a corner.

The prince's men in the golden tower had already signaled the rest to begin their move. They removed their armor and helmets and headed to the guest quarters. They got on their horses, which the night before they had ordered to be brought to them at sunrise. They joined Prince Vallusin who was heading towards the gate.

The unusual screeching of the worm and the barking of Saiparak had caught the attention of the guards on the two fortification walls.

They noticed that the tower guards were missing, and they rushed to inform their superiors.

At that point, the gatekeepers opened the gate for the prince and his entourage and let them depart as they had been instructed, supposedly to facilitate their early hunting venture.

In the meantime, the bewildered tower guards were awakened to the sound of a blast that shook the earth. In a state of confusion they did not remember what had happened to them during the night.

Septabliss, on his way to the fortress, heard the unusual screeching, and then the explosion. He rushed in and went straight to the golden tower. Allusin was missing! He called her several times, but there was no answer. No sound came now from the worm's chamber. Remembering the horrid noise, he hesitated before the door for a few seconds. His trembling legs could hardly drag his body forward. Cautiously he stepped into the worm's chamber. It was dark and the air was filled with stench. He leaned against the wall to keep his balance. It was slimy. When his eyes got used to the dark, he saw the worm's three heads on the floor with no corpse attached to them. Then, Septabliss's body slid to the floor, which was covered with the pieces of the worm's exploded stomach. His mind switched off for good.

Amaease was hiding in one of the underground passages. Through a secret door connected to Allusin's quarters, he entered Allusin's bedroom. He went to the window and saw the ropes hanging down; he pulled them up, hid them under the bed, and closed the window. Then he went to the worm's chamber. The worm's eyes were open as if they were staring at him. He shivered. He had never suspected such a metamorphosis in the worm. He looked around and saw Septabliss. Question after question jammed his mind. How could a stupid man like Septabliss deceive him? How could the maiden keep the secret for so long? What did Peerbabu get out of all this? Why did Peerbabu insist that he not join Septabliss's guests last night? Who were those people? A violent rage invaded his body.

Vengeance was boiling in his heart. He had to get to work to control the new situation.

He held Septabliss's head and emptied the contents of a small bottle of potion into his mouth and waited a few minutes. Septabliss's body began to shake. His paralyzed limbs crumbled to the floor. Amaease carefully lifted Septabliss's body and took him to the other room. He removed Septabliss's soiled garments, cleaned him, and wrapped his body in a large white sheet. Amaease threw the clothes into the worm's chamber, locked the door, and put the key into his pocket and carried Septabliss out in his arms.

At last, Septabliss was in a position that pleased Amaease. Septabliss was a limp body without a mind at his disposal. This achievement was very gratifying to Amaease, and it appeased his anger.

There was a commotion outside. Baffled, the fortress's residents were all outside, questioning each other and searching for answers. The guards were also shocked when they saw Amaease exiting with Septabliss's body from the dragon's quarters. Nobody had seen Amaease passing through that door, but all had heard what he had said to Allusin. A deadly silence fell upon the fortress! Septabliss's body was heavy, but Amaease, during those concentrated moments, had developed such extraordinary power that he could have easily carried even the whole tower. Poised, Amaease went downstairs and walked towards the platform. Only the sound of his heavy steps counted the passing time. He asked for a stretcher to be brought out and respectfully put Septabliss's body on it. In a somber tone he began to address the people:

"My good people! The sound that you heard was Allusin's departure to heaven. Before her journey she informed me that she was going to join constellation Draco. It was her reward for the dedicated service she had rendered to the holy Bouriaz.

"Before her departure Allusin said to me that the divine dragon wished the special meal served today to be his last. Thus, the entrance to the holy dragon's tower will be sealed for good. My dear old friend

Septabliss was heartbroken by his daughter's sudden departure. He will remain in the state of shock as long as he refuses to accept her divine destiny. The holy dragon will redeem his health and forgive his sin, if my friend repents.

"I want two of the commanders to take the news to Vantu. He is the one who should decide what to do with his father. Now I need to go into seclusion and pray for my friend Septabliss and this town."

Then he gravely walked away without looking at anyone and went straight to his room in the temple. No one dared to ask him the many questions they had on their minds. What he left behind in the people's hearts was more a sense of fear than of respect. No one knew what to do, as no one was in charge. The uncertainty began to grow. The news spread and the people of Kolallan learned about the events of the day. The mayor and other influential men got together to discuss the situation. They all knew that Vantu was not capable of replacing his father. Recently they had not even been happy with Septabliss himself but had tolerated him because of Allusin. The more they talked, the clearer it became that no one other than Amaease was fit to take control. In order to prevent any interruptions in the chain of command, that very evening they went to Amaease and asked him to accept the leadership.

"It is not an easy decision. I am a holy man, and my place is right here at the temple. I need to consult with the heavenly authorities, as I have done for many years. I was sent here to save this town. I was the one who taught Allusin how to receive the heavenly messages, and I helped Septabliss to perform his duty and win the war, but unfortunately, as of late he had become disobedient and refused to follow the holy dragon's wishes. We have witnessed his fate. If the heavens will commission me to rule this city, I will need your undivided support, as well as that of the army. This town needs to be disciplined to fight our enemy. There are dark forces conspiring to destroy Kolallan. They want to get their hands on your treasures. Septabliss was a fool to let such conspirators be entertained at the fortress. You probably have seen or heard that the parade you saw yesterday was sheer sorcery. The treasures brought by the imposter turned out to be rubbish. Even the exotic animals were only crumbled pieces of paper and metal. By black magic they intend to ruin us. Our holy dragon may not roar again as long as we let this kind of wizardry work in our town. He demands that we resist the force ourselves to prove our unrelenting dedication to him. If I am told to accept this challenge I shall issue a proclamation tomorrow. Otherwise I shall advise you as to who would be the best candidate."

His words reached people fast and worried them, as they were convinced that there was no one as capable as Amaease to take the lead. They gathered at the temple and prayed for Amaease's acceptance. The news was reported to him on an hourly basis. He was elated to hear that things were working according to his plan. He was getting the town ready to back him up, so that with their support he could defeat Peerbabu.

The next morning he sent out this proclamation:

"Brave people of Kolallan! Last night the holy dragon appeared in my dream as I had requested in my prayers. He ordered me to take up this challenge because our very existence depends upon it. The dark force is operating amongst us in many different ways. We need to find out how it functions in order to stop it. It is the desire of holy Bouriaz that you be vigilant. Watch your friends, neighbors, and all who come to town. Black magic preys on your innocence and breeds on your mistakes. No one is allowed to leave home after dark. On the appointed days gatherings will be permitted only in the temple and in the fortress in order to prevent any plots against our sacred dragon. Words, thoughts, and deeds which are not in harmony with our present order should be reported immediately. But above all we need an army to protect the city. The fortress is quite secure, but the innocent people of Kolallan, who have become the target of the dark force, are not secure. Therefore, all young men over fourteen will be drafted to undergo training. I assure you that we will, in no time, defeat our enemy and celebrate our victory. I am happy to announce that the holy dragon Bouriaz will be pleased to accept your offerings from tomorrow on."

The next day people, as always, stood in line to visit the dragon. The dragon roared when a middle-aged woman, who was the first visitor, looked through the Kot. She was so frightened she nearly fainted. The same thing happened with the second and the third and the fourth. The fifth one in line refused to look and just left his offerings. The line broke apart and the bewildered crowd scattered. Amaease was working in Septabliss's office when he heard the roars. Immediately he sensed that there was something unusual going on. Peerbabu had tricked him! The dragon would roar each time someone looked through the Kot. He went out to meet with people.

"Oh my good people! Our gracious dragon has decided to tell you right away whether your offerings have been accepted or not. Whoever is roared at will be the one rewarded. But I forgot to mention in my proclamation that although from today on the dragon will receive you every day, he will not accept more than five visitors a day. In order to facilitate your visits, someone at the door will write your name and will tell you when to come. Travelers who are passing through will have the first priority. In this way no one will have to stand in line for hours or go back empty-handed. There will be no more visits today."

When Amaease was back in his office, he muttered, "Pretty soon Peerbabu will run out of his dull tricks, and I will be in charge of an army that will conquer the whole country. He is a pitiful old man with a scary appearance who does not dare to show his face in public. He made a big mistake choosing me as his opponent. He started the war, but I am the one who will finish it."

16

I took Peerbabu a couple of days to bring Allusin back to health. Prince Vallusin spent most of his time at her bedside, comforting her whenever she opened her eyes and asked about Saiparak.

"Saiparak is in good hands," the prince assured Allusin. "Peerbabu will show you where Saiparak is when you are well enough to leave your bed."

One night when she had the strength to walk, Peerbabu took her to the roof and said, "When I brought Saiparak to you, do you remember the story I told you about him?"

"Yes, I do," replied Allusin. "You said that he was a magic star and it changed its form three times a month."

"You have good memory. Follow the direction of my finger! There he is with his constant companion. He has traveled from one side of the Milky Way to the other."

"You mean I will never see him again?" cried Allusin.

"I mean that you can always see him in the sky. At this juncture his mission on Earth has ended, but like his constant companion in the sky, forever he will remain at your side."

"I shall always miss him. He was such a loyal friend. That wicked worm that brought so much misery into my life must have killed Saiparak; strange that I was so delighted when I discovered it. I wonder why I saved that little creature that later became a monster," said Allusin.

"It was the dark force that tricked you. How could you have known that mentioning the name Vallusin would have placed the evil force so close in your life! My dear girl, let us look at the bright side as well. Spindles brought you misery, yet spindles set you free. It was your long ropes that gave me the idea of the escape through the window. Without your ropes many lives would have been lost. True, one part of the monster's body is dead, but its depraved soul is very much alive and at work. Evil can never be totally eradicated, but it can be weakened and reduced to a point that it does not have the power to cause great destruction. As long as the future looks brighter than the past, we should know that the dark force is weaker than it was before. This is called hope. Your heart, better than anyone else's, responds to this bliss. I am sure that Prince Vallusin is missing your company. Shall we go downstairs and join him?"

Allusin was greatly comforted by Peerbabu's words. Her eyes were lit up and the smile was returned to her lips.

"You look completely recovered, my sweet," exclaimed Vallusin. "Peerbabu's healing becomes stronger with age."

"Before we set the groundwork for war, I would like to begin preparing for your wedding," said Peerbabu. "You choose the approximate date and I will choose the exact day and time that will be the most auspicious."

"I would like to get married as soon as you can arrange it, Peerbabu," said the prince. "I would like to leave the day after the wedding, because I do not want to give Amaease more time to establish himself as a leader. I must go to King Vima for help, but before that I will accompany Nerssey's men to join their regiment and I will ask him to contact the other commanders to be standing by for my order."

"This is a wise plan," confirmed Peerbabu, "Do you intend to attack the fortress first or the castles?"

"First we must attack the two castles to rescue many of the prisoners they hold," answered Prince Vallusin. "As you mentioned before, there are a large number of discontented soldiers among Amaease's men that may join us in the fight. With the two castles fallen, we shall have enough soldiers to attack the fortress."

"Unfortunately a bloodbath is inevitable, but hopefully it shall end quickly," said Peerbabu. "Their force is great, but they cannot sustain it for long. They are like owls that fly fast but only short distances. Let us not talk further about war and celebrate a wedding that has long been delayed!"

The ceremony was performed in a room in the center of which a fire burned. The room was decorated with aromatic flowers and branches of spruce and thyme.

The bride was dressed in white muslin and wore a garland of fresh myrtle over a veil and carried a wildflower bouquet; she shone like a full moon. The bridegroom wore white pleated pants, a tight white tunic, and a gold girdle. On his head was a gold headband inlaid with precious stones—he looked like a sun on a midsummer day. Cross-legged, they sat on two cushions. In front of them was a large white cotton cloth covered with rose petals. At the end of that stood a tall mirror with two candelabra at each side. In its center, upon a square green woolen cloth, sat a glass bowl filled with rose water. Surrounding the bowl were dishes of dried sweet fruits, rice and almond cookies, and tiny aromatic white candies. Peerbabu performed their nuptial ceremony.

O Lord of light, brightness, and glory!
All ruling, beneficent, and holy!
I invoke your blessings towards Allusin and Vallusin!
Grant them to be of one thought, of one speech,
And of one deed in marriage!
Let them use the strength of truth in their words!
Let them share the luminous space of wisdom in their
    thoughts!

Let them be the guardians of justice and peace!
Stay by the side of Prince Vallusin, the gallant warrior,
Let his conscience be ever struggling for mercy and charity!
Help the purest of hearts, Allusin, to bring forth offspring,
Boys and girls, many and good, many and fair, many and
    bright!
Let no deathly sickness enter their bodies!
Let no uncleanness enter their home!
Grant them long life, much joy, with eyes of love!

Then he held their hands and led them around the fire seven times. He gave them nectar with white basil seeds to drink. There was music and singing and dancing. It was on the twenty-ninth of the month, a very propitious day for Prince Vallusin and Allusin to be married.

17

oon after the wedding, Prince Vallusin had an audience with King Vima. He told him the story of Septabliss and the worm worshippers:

"The worm is dead, however the fortification is not easy to conquer with a small army. To defeat them I will need more men. Before my departure I heard that Septabliss was paralyzed and out of the picture. Now Amaease is in command. By planting fear in people's hearts, he is manipulating them and forcing them to unite. He has put the city on a high state of alert. His soldiers are patrolling the streets around the clock. To stop the deception we must act quickly before it spreads throughout the country. People are flooding from near and far to see the dragon and offer their life savings to the dragon. Besides, the wealth he has accumulated would be of great use to our treasury."

"In a short period of time, Prince Vallusin, you seem to have grown from a bold young soldier to a wise warrior," said the king. "I have no doubt that Peerbabu has chosen the right man for the task. You will be provided with a big enough army to defeat Amaease. I myself was planning to take care of this wicked creature. After the lengthy war the treasury does need to be replenished. But kings should never be bribed, my prince! Did not Peerbabu teach you that?"

"Your Majesty!" said Prince Vallusin. "My tongue is still not learned enough to carry the wisdom of Peerbabu. My words are not elaborate enough for presentation before the king, nor plain enough not to be misunderstood. I am taught honesty is appreciated by great kings."

"Your good intention is well received," said the king in a fatherly tone. "It is wise to be truthful and straightforward with your king. You carry signs of a wise ruler, which are modesty, fairness, and courage to confront evil. May you never fail to bring goodness to the people and to please Heaven!"

Late one chilly evening, during Prince Vallusin's absence, Peerbabu paid a secret visit to Prince Sarabaress in prison. The prince was delighted when he heard the news that Prince Vallusin was alive and had married Allusin. He wanted to know every little detail of their plans and laughed heartily like a child.

Peerbabu informed Prince Sarabaress about Prince Vallusin's plans for the upcoming battles.

"It is helpful to know," said Prince Sarabaress, "that there is one secret passage in my bedroom and a similar one in Prince Vallusin's bedroom in the other castle. They are under the fireplace, and their openings are two miles away outside the castles in the woods next to an oak tree with initials B. D. on it. Through those passages your men could invade both castles from within."

The next week following that visit, Peerbabu decided to check the underground passages and the secret doors of the fortress. It was cloudy and dark but the torches were burning bright all around the fortress. He walked through the fortress, trying not to attract the guards' attention. He sensed the presence of an intense negative energy, which increased with every step he took as he approached the towers. It was as if the concentrated force in the pillars of the seven towers were arrogantly challenging heaven's authority.

He was drawn to the golden tower and to Allusin's room. There he was! Amaease was on the floor near the fireplace curled up under a blanket.

Amaease felt a presence and quickly stood up. "So it is you again!" he said coldly, without fear.

Peerbabu stared at him.

"I knew that you would eventually find me here. Are you here for another deal?"

Peerbabu was quiet.

"There will be no deal this time," Amaease continued, "unless I dictate it. The reason I accepted your offer was because I needed to buy time for myself, which I did. You thought you could ruin me by that sick joke you played on me?"

"No. I needed to buy a little time as well, which I did," said Peerbabu. "But it has scared people away just the same, has it not? The disappointment of not being rewarded has kept people away. Is your revenue rapidly decreasing?"

"Very soon I will not be dependent upon that income anymore. Your tricks are becoming obsolete and boring. I can handle all your wizardry. Actually, there is nothing left that I cannot handle anymore. Now that you are here, you may answer this question: Why were you so interested in saving Allusin? Are you hiding her in your tower? I never understood why you went to so much trouble to save that girl."

"One good soul saved fights off a thousand evil ones."

"Ha! You still believe that fools win, do you not? Fools are victims of their own foolishness. Born as fools, they repeat the same mistake a thousand times. If you put your magic into action for me instead, together we shall conquer the entire earth. Not that I cannot achieve my goal without you, but it may facilitate the process," said Amaease, using his usual condescending tone.

"Are you trying to bribe me, Amaease? You are a pathetic sight. You have fallen to the bestial level that is beyond salvation. There is no human quality left in you."

Amaease grinned. "Does that scare you, Peerbabu? I am beyond your reach. You cannot touch me ever again! You too will soon fall into my traps."

"Innocent and helpless people are your victims. You feed on them. Continually reliving your bitter childhood experiences makes the deep hatred in your heart grow. Your soul is famished, not your body. The greedy worm's head will be with you for the rest of your life. No one will trust you for long, because your heart is closed to all and has become incapable of accepting trust. Septabliss was not as totally evil as you are. Being greedy and vain, he prepared the foundation for you to rise. He helped you to get where you are now, but gradually you destroyed him. In your eyes, everyone who has power is an obstacle and must be eliminated, because you want to be in total control. There will come a day that you cannot tolerate or trust even yourself. You will devour the jealous Amaease. Did it ever occur to you why you never look into a mirror?"

Amaease felt a sharp blow to his stomach, but he controlled himself and said, "You are up to another trick. I told you your tricks do not work any more. I am a real man. You are a dead ghost without a body. I wonder whether you have any reflection in the mirror."

"I am the mirror, you fool! Even if I were a ghost, no matter in whose body you hide or into whose mind you crawl, your own monsters and giants will forever haunt you, disrupting your actions and obstructing your advancement. You will never escape the rotten pit and will never be freed from the beatings of your sisters. You are not even half a man. You have chosen to remain evil."

Amaease could not contain the rage that stormed his body. He felt like striking Peerbabu with all his force. Slowly he took a few steps forward toward Peerbabu, concentrating his energy.

Suddenly Peerbabu had a flash in his mind. He saw a guard put a few drops of a potion in Prince Sarabaress's wineglass. He put the glass on a tray with the meal, carried it to his cell, and left it on the table for him. Then the guard went away and locked the door behind him. Prince Sarabaress lifted the glass to drink the wine.

Peerbabu waved his right hand in the air as if he were hitting something and shouted, "NO!" In his vision he saw the wineglass thrown to the floor.

Peerbabu immediately left for the prison.

Amaease froze. He thought that Peerbabu's hand motion and his yell were reactions to his own threatening behavior. He had scared Peerbabu away! He was beyond himself with ecstasy. He jumped up and down like a monkey, making weird noises. Experiencing joy was quite bizarre to him. Peerbabu's sudden appearance in the temple that night had left a deep mark of insecurity in him. He felt Peerbabu's presence everywhere, as if he were under his scrutiny at all times. All the laws and orders that he had issued were based upon obstructing Peerbabu from intervening with his future plans. It made him feel triumphant thinking he had frightened Peerbabu away.

"Now he is the one who has to hide in that pit. Fearing this humiliating experience will keep him out of the public eye for good. The road to glory is paved for me and I will be crowned in no time."

As Prince Sarabaress was wondering about the incident of the broken glass, Peerbabu appeared before him.

"I am glad you came, Peerbabu. Was it you who denied me a cup of wine tonight?"

Peerbabu nodded and said, "Amaease is preparing for war. His passion for destruction is accelerating by the minute. The enormous negative energy he has collected is dangerous. His army and the people of Kolallan have all rallied to fight against an unknown source of black magic. Yielding to this fear, they are united to fight against this hidden force. He has begun to execute his plan. The reason he did not get rid of you after he captured the castle was because you reminded him of his father. But now he cannot afford to be sentimental. His self-importance is highly inflated and he is totally consumed by his sick ambition. Tonight I could feel the destructive power at work in every inch of the fortress. You and the other prisoners are no longer safe here. He has issued your death sentence and may have done the same for the other prisoners in both castles. He is merciless."

"If we release the prisoners, we could take back the castle," said Prince Sarabaress. "The guard who brought me the wine was a new one. I had never seen him before. I had always had good conversations with the old one. He repeatedly said that he was unhappy here, as were many other guards. Most of them wanted to go back to their lands. They used to be paid on a regular basis, but when Amaease left the castle and never returned for a visit, the chief commander stopped the payments. The guard thought that the chief commander was pocketing the money himself. The corruption has already begun to show its face. When my soldiers see me, they will be ready to fight, though I do not know in what shape they are now. The guard told me that the meal which was served to them used to be ample, but such is not the case anymore."

"We need to act tonight," said Peerbabu. "If you conduct the fight here, I shall take care of the other castle. I need to go to Sanrod and lead Nerssey's men through the underground tunnel to the castle. They will get here after dawn. If the same sentiment exists among the guards in Prince Vallusin's castle, then we can count on our victory. I will check on the guards and return here immediately."

There were only a couple of men on guard on the towers. The chief commander was snoring and the rest were sleeping comfortably. Peerbabu opened the doors of the cells and the armories and departed.

Silently, Prince Sarabaress woke the prisoners one by one and described his plan. The soldiers were thrilled to see him alive and well. Enthusiastically they picked up arms and quietly overcame the half-asleep guards. The chief commander and all his soldiers were locked up.

Peerbabu showed the entrance of the tunnel to Nerssey, to whom Peerbabu had already given a sketch of the castle. The sun was about to rise. Peerbabu went to Prince Vallusin's room. It was the same room that the prince's parents used to sleep in, and now the chief commander was using it. Unlike the commander of the other castle, this one seemed to have taken his post of command seriously and was checking on the guards. Peerbabu opened the entrance, which was hidden under the ashes of the fireplace, helped the soldiers enter the room, then left. Though Nerssey's men tried to capture the castle with not much bloodshed, they could not release the prisoners in time to take part in the fight. The fight got out of control.

There were many dead and injured on both sides, but within a few hours the castle fell into the hands of Nerssey's men. By that time, Prince Vallusin's army had also arrived and had surrounded the castles, so that no one could take the news to Kolallan.

Amaease was expecting to hear the daily news from his commanders in the castles. Because he did not receive his usual briefings, he dispatched two pages to find out what was happening. When they did not return, he became suspicious and sent a group of forty soldiers to investigate the matter. As the soldiers did not notice any changes in the castles, they entered. They were captured as well.

By the following nightfall when none of them had returned, Amaease grew extremely anxious. He became restless and angry and could not imagine what had gone wrong. He ordered his army to be ready to leave town. He left one third of his men in the fortress.

The king's army under Prince Vallusin's command had camped not very far from Kolallan.

To squeeze Amaease's men in between, one regiment of Prince Vallusin's troops surrounded the fortress and began its assault early in the morning, while another one, which had entered the fortress through the underground tunnel the night before, attacked from within. The narrow passage had seven branches, which opened into the seven towers through secret doors. Peerbabu had already left the doors open.

The two armies met outside the city. The battle was fierce and brutal.

Atop a hilltop, Amaease, upon a white horse, was vigilantly watching the battle. When his army began to retreat he rushed back to the fortress. There he saw Prince Vallusin's soldiers swarming out of the secret doors into the towers. Right away he knew that his men were losing ground and he should not linger there. Swiftly he rode to the temple and went to his room. He loaded four bags of gold coins and precious stones, changed his horse, and left the temple on a black stallion. He galloped toward the horizon where the sun was setting; his figure began to shrink as he rode away. Frantically he was searching his mind to find a refuge wherein he could collect his runaway thoughts, but the only flashing one in his memory was a dark smelly pit that he detested to visit again.

Amaease's army retreated and entered Kolallan. They dragged the fight into streets and homes to use women and children as human shields. The carnage was appalling. Elders prayed, women screamed, children cried, birds flew away, and dogs barked, but nothing helped the helpless. All rescue efforts were in vain. Fire broke out and the houses went up in flames. The unleashed evil was stronger and the savagery more violent on both sides than Peerbabu had predicted.

The sun witnessed the collapse of the golden dome and the scattered body of the fake dragon. Not much was left of the other towers except the naked tall pillars, which were still standing, devoid of purpose. Vultures in great numbers began to guard the destroyed watchtowers. In the white tower broken jars were scattered all over. Honey mixed with blood covered the bodies of the maidens who had once served the dragon. People by the hundreds stormed the fortress in frenzy anxious to find out whether their loved ones inside were still alive.

But strangely enough, the worm's chamber had remained untouched.

Prince Vallusin ordered its walls to be brought down. The stinking odor was so strong that some fled the scene. Finally the worm's heads were exposed. People screamed in disgust and turned their faces. For the first time they faced the deception by which most of them had lost their savings and even the lives of their family members. During the rest of the day people went to the fortress to look at the worm's heads and the torn pieces of the fake golden dragon's body.

The disillusioned town went into a deadly silence. No footstep could be heard in the alleys and squares. People remained in shock for weeks. Families mourned the loss of their young soldiers, who had died for a false cause. The elders mourned the innocence lost. The young were confused, resentful, and angry. People walked about agitated, each accusing everyone else for having been led into deception.

Prince Vallusin let the people mourn their dead for forty days, after which he announced a public gathering in the largest square of Kolallan.

"My countrymen! Though the outcome of the battle was wickedness destroyed, in the eyes of Heaven it was not a victory. Neither is it in my eyes. Ruined houses can be rebuilt, but lives lost are gone forever. A triumphant heart is the one that does not allow darkness to gain strength and rule the soul. The insignia of the dragon can be scourged from your clothes, from your walls, and from your doors, but to remove it from a greedy heart is difficult. This battle we won, so it seems, but the real battle is yet ahead. We need to help each other to build everlasting watchtowers in our souls. We need each other's help, we need each other's understanding, and we need to forgive in order to heal, which is difficult. But if loss and suffering do not bring us together, the opportunity for a dignified existence is lost in this lifetime. Repentance in words is meaningless. Closing one's eyes to wickedness is ruthlessness. Acting without believing is worthless. We need to be truthful in our minds, our words, and our deeds simultaneously."

It took years for the people of Kolallan to cleanse their souls from the deception that Septabliss and Amaease had brought. With time the greed and the desire for the superficialities of life slowly disappeared. There was a young generation who had not known any other divinity than the golden dragon. It was not easy for the elderly either, facing the cruel deceit that had shattered the foundations of their lives. The feelings of guilt, which stemmed from having worshipped the dark force of evil, made their hearts heavy. People celebrated no longer, but mourned, often repenting their lust. But as time passed, gradually people freed themselves of their grief and anger and began to heal. They started celebrating life in a meaningful way, seeking simplicity and harmony, following the order of nature.

18

ne of the greatest celebrations in the country was always five days in the month of November. Throughout that period people went to temples to pray, and at home they honored their ancestors' souls, believing that in those five days they would descend to earth, bringing them health and happiness. There was housecleaning; and food and drinks of all kind on tables to be given to the poor.

To the rituals performed during that period in the land, the people of Kolallan added one session of singing and dancing. The purpose was to remember the deception, which had brought them so much pleasure but had caused much greater pain.

Friends and families sat on the floor in a circle, clapping. A chorus of five maidens wearing all white stood in a smaller circle facing the audience. In the center there was a young man wearing black pants and a red satin shirt, dancing and singing with a tambourine:

> Here's a story you behold!
> Septabliss found a worm,
> Bringing fortune, silver, and gold.

Chorus:
Septabliss hoards and hoards.

Septabliss hailed the worm.
His tail was long, he said.
Chorus in mock surprise:
It had no tail!

Septabliss adored the worm.
His tongue was red, he said.
Chorus in mock surprise:
It had no tongue!

Septabliss praised the worm.
His legs were short, he said.
Chorus in mock surprise:
It had no legs!

Septabliss prayed to the worm.
His head was large, he said.
Chorus in mock surprise:
It had three heads!

Septabliss to fortress went,
Riding on the crawling worm.
Young men hailed the crawling worm.
Chorus mimicking:
Young men hailed the crawling worm.

Women waved to the crawling worm.
Chorus mimicking:
Women waved to the crawling worm.

Only children cried, scared!

Chorus mimicking:
Only children cried, scared.

Septabliss with no legs,
One fat tummy, three big heads,
A dragon was he?
He was not!
Chorus:
He was not!
Chorus, holding their noses in disgust.
Septabliss was a stinky clown!

Before Prince Vallusin became the ruling king, Peerbabu met with him once more.

"Peerbabu, I have launched an extensive search to locate Amaease," said Prince Vallusin, "but it has been to no avail. No one has any knowledge of his whereabouts. Where do you think he is hiding? Will we ever confront him again?"

"For the time being he has gone into oblivion," said Peerbabu, "a wanderer in the wilderness of the world of darkness, but the moment he hoards enough energy to fight and find another prey to operate through, he will resurface. I have no doubt that soon he will appear on my path again! Evil, as you well know, continues its existence amongst us, but it is up to you now to prevent him from strengthening his roots in your kingdom."

"By being a just ruler, combating deceit and ignorance!" said Prince Vallusin.

"A lesson well learned, my Lord!" said Peerbabu, and by these words, he disappeared.

After King Vima died, Prince Vallusin and Princess Allusin became king and queen of the land. During their reign the country prospered and enjoyed a long peaceful period. Travelers who journeyed through the land referred to it as Paradise. Allusin and Vallusin became a legend and forever stayed in the folk stories of that land.

Their names still resonate in a song that children sing in Kolallan. Whenever they anticipate arrivals of loved ones, they jump up and down cheerfully, mentioning the name of that person, and recite:

Oh Allusin!
Oh Vallusin!
The moon, glimmering!
The sun, glittering!
Riding in chariots
Horses thundering,
Hasten to me!
My dear . . .

About the Author

Homa A. Garemani, a writer, poet, and translator, was born and raised in Iran. She studied the German language in Germany and earned a graduate degree from the University of Tehran, majoring in German literature.

She immigrated to the United States in 1976 and ever since has lived in California. She is the widow of A. M. Garemani and a grandmother of two to her only son.

Hampton Roads Publishing Company

... for the evolving human spirit

Hampton Roads Publishing Company
publishes books on a variety of subjects,
including metaphysics, health,
visionary fiction, and other related topics.

For a copy of our latest catalog, call toll-free
(800) 766-8009, or send your name and address to:

Hampton Roads Publishing Company, Inc.
1125 Stoney Ridge Road
Charlottesville, VA 22902

e-mail: hrpc@hrpub.com
www.hrpub.com